DEDICATION

In Loving Memory

of

John and Jeanette 'Betty' Kennedy

Two very special friends
and great supporters of our book world.

Reunited at last, never forgotten, loved always

REGRETS

HELLION MC
BOOK 2

AVA MANELLO

PROLOGUE

S ue

I can barely see the road ahead of me for the tears I'm crying. I've been such a bloody fool. I really believed that there was something special between Jackson and me. After losing Elvis, I thought I'd always be on my own, and I swore away from having anything to do with bikers, but then I met Jackson. He gave my topsy-turvy world balance, a reason to get out of bed every morning, and then eventually my smile returned. I'll always miss Elvis, but I know he'd have wanted me to move on.

When Jackson mentioned he wanted to talk, I thought he was going to suggest us moving in together. I never expected he was going to destroy everything. He spouted a load of bullshit about doing this for me, and that I deserved better. I know deep down that he's just scared of commitment, but how do I make him realize that?

Even spending the day with Teresa and the baby over in Severed hasn't helped lift the cloud that's settled over me.

Things had been so great between us these past few months, especially the last few weeks when Eve's friends came over from England. I'd thought we were closer than ever, but turns out, Jackson was just looking for a way to let me down easily.

"We need to talk." How many relationships have those words destroyed? Four little words that carry so much weight, especially when you're obviously a naïve fool like me and thought they meant something altogether different.

I've been half listening to 3 Doors Down and as I hear the intro of the next song, it breaks my heart a little more - 'What's Left'. I used to joke that if I ever dumped Jackson, I'd do it by text and send him the link to this song. The lyrics rip my heart out every time I hear them, they're so poignant. It's all about after the break when you're sorting out all the memories and trying to let them go. It's a song that's always had an effect on me, especially after losing Elvis so suddenly.

I think Teresa was relieved about the split. She's never come out and verbalized it, but she's never really accepted how quickly I moved on from her father. It wasn't intentional; I hadn't planned on meeting someone; I hadn't even wanted to.

But Jackson came into my life, and as I got to know him, I knew I couldn't let him go.

Eve's always been my advocate with Teresa, and as hard work as Teresa can be some days, thanks to her strong personality, I've always had a soft spot for her. The poor girl has lost both her parents, her mum to cancer back in England and then her dad was murdered here in Australia. She came so close to losing her husband as well; she'd gone into labor believing he was dead.

She's so strong. I wish I had a fraction of her strength. I was over the moon when she asked me to step up and help her with the new baby; I thought that after losing Elvis I'd lose all my friends I'd made through him in Severed as well. I should have known better. Bikers are all about family, well, these bikers are. We lost Elvis because not all MC's feel like that; he was caught in the crossfire when they tried to kill Eve. It all sounds so complicated and far-fetched now. Eve had witnessed a murder, and Carnal MC believed the only good witness was a dead witness and did their best to achieve that outcome.

Poor Eve had come over from England for her best friend's wedding and ended up nearly losing her own life on more than one occasion. She was saved when Severed MC took her in and made her one of their own, the same way they took me in. Prez made it clear that as long as I was happy, and Jackson looked out for me, they had no problem with me seeing someone from another MC and wanted me to know that if I ever needed it, I'd always have a home with them in Severed. Looks like I may have to take them up on that now. The memories here are raw and new which makes them more painful than the memories I ran from in Severed.

I moved away after Elvis was shot. The bad memories far outweighed the good. That's how I met Jackson, along with a couple of his friends. He'd helped me carry the boxes from the truck to the house on the day I moved in. I'd chosen Maldon because it was close enough to stay in touch with my Severed family, but far enough away that I wouldn't bump into them every day.

I'm going to miss Rebel, Jackson's daughter. The poor girl had been abandoned at the gates of Hellion MC as a baby and Jackson and the guys had raised her as their own. That's the thing with a breakup. You don't just lose the person you love; you lose their family and friends that you fell in love with too. As hard as it is to lose someone when they die, you don't lose everyone around them as well.

I give myself a shake; I need to pull myself out of this pity party. I'm fifty-two years old for God's sake. I should know better than to be sitting here bawling like a teenager. I need to keep my focus on the road, not on what might have been.

It's a pleasant enough drive between Maldon and Severed, mainly back roads with some long open stretches and not too much traffic at this time of night. I haven't seen another vehicle for the last fifteen minutes. Dusk has always been one of my favorite times of day, the glow of the setting sun turning the whole sky a hazy red, a good time to sit on my deck with a glass of wine and reflect on my day with Jackson. I stop myself. That's not going to happen again, but there's nothing to stop me sitting there with a glass of wine on my own.

There's an eighteen-wheeler coming towards me and I shudder. I've never been a fan of them, and I have this irrational fear that one of them is going to roll over and land on me as I drive past. It's stupid, I know, but I can't help it. I laugh when the line in the next track on the CD tells me 'The long road awaits'. It's almost as though this CD is reading my mood.

As I near the oncoming truck, I press my foot a little harder on the accelerator. I'm not speeding, but I want to get past it as quickly as possible. As I come level with the cab, the driver, a slightly older guy, waves at me. Before I can pass him an explosion of noise fills the air, and a look of horror crosses his face. The cab of the truck veers onto my side of the road and I try to swerve away from him, but I'm too slow. There's a horrendously loud grinding noise as metal hits metal and my car is pushed along the road. In what feels like slow motion, my car starts to tip over. This stretch of road may be lovely to drive along, but in a moment of clarity, I remember that my side of the road is the one with the drop off. The car seems to tumble over and over forever, before finally landing on its roof. The windscreen in front of me is shattered and half the height it is supposed to be. It's not tears blinding my vision now, it's blood. I can feel the warm sticky trail it's leaving down my cheek.

My last thought before everything goes dark is Jackson.

CHAPTER ONE

J **ackson**

The guy in the filling station gives me an odd look as I hand over the cash for my gas and the flowers I'm taking to Rebel's. I'm guessing he doesn't get many leather clad bikers buying floral gifts. I nod my thanks as I accept my change, and I have to say I feel a little sad that something as simple as buying a woman flowers is seen as unusual these days. What happened to good old-fashioned courting?

I stow the flowers in the pannier of my bike and take a moment to just enjoy the early evening. It's been a hot day and thankfully it's cooled off a touch. Rebel's invited me over and is going to throw a couple of steaks on the grill and we'll be able to enjoy them out on her deck. Unlike some of my brothers I won't feel emasculated if she's doing the grilling, instead I'll appreciate the view and someone taking care of me.

I 'm pretty sure that Rebel is going to interrogate me about what happened with Sue, and why I broke up with her. I'm not sure if I can explain it to her, but I do know that she'll give me grief. I'm not quite sure when Sue became a permanent feature in my life, it's kind of just crept up on me I guess. One minute I was on my own, and the next she was there, slowly ingratiating herself into my daily routine. She never put me under any pressure to make what we had anything more than a casual affair and I appreciated that, after all these years I don't think I'm cut out for settling down. I'm too accustomed to my ways to share a home with a woman, although not that old that I can't appreciate a sleepover.

Sue's good company, we're very compatible in bed and she tolerates me being part of the club, although I wouldn't say she embraces it. She's familiar with club life. It's not the fact that I'm a biker that bothers her, just that violence seems to attract itself to an MC, even the good ones. It's how she lost her man. He was shot when a rival MC were out for revenge. She moved here to get away from the biker life and then met me. She used to say that it was ironic, whereas I would say it was good luck on her part as she ended up with me. I was getting too comfortable with Sue, too set in my ways and for some reason that scared me. I could tell from the shock on her face that when I stated we needed to talk, she was expecting a totally different outcome. The week before she'd suggested moving in with her, we were spending so much time together it made more sense than keeping up two separate houses. That's when the panic set in and I called an end to us. I miss her like crazy, but I did it for her. She deserves better than me.

There's a wail of sirens as a fire engine and ambulance race past, someone's having a bad day. I shake the melancholy thoughts from my mind as I turn the key and feel the power of the bike rumble underneath me. Time to go face the Spanish Inquisition from my daughter.

Looks like the emergency services are heading out of Maldon on the same road as me, and I slow down so as not to attract unwanted attention. As I get closer its apparent that I won't be using this road this evening, there's a huge red eighteen-wheeler skewed across the road blocking it. The cab is damaged and all along one side there are ugly scrapes where bare metal shows through.

I pull the bike to a halt and put the kickstand down before approaching the nearest policeman to offer help. From the way the activity is centered around the drop off and the black skid marks on the road surface it looks like someone has gone over the edge. I take a sharp inhale of breath, that's a steep drop and I just hope they're in a decent vehicle to protect them.

The officer welcomes my assistance, and I'm directed to help set up and secure the guide ropes with the fire crew so the medic and lead fireman can descend and see what the situation is below. It's eerily quiet as they reach the bottom of the ropes. It seems like everyone around us is holding their breath, the silent flashing of the emergency lights casting a surreal blue and red glow over everything.

A radio crackles into life and most of what I hear is coded or gibberish, but the call for the air ambulance is clear. Whoever is down there has survived the wreck, but barely. While we wait for the helicopter, we keep busy sending down medical equipment as a policeman starts measuring up the scene. It's clear from the way he's methodically working that they think this accident is going to result in a fatality.

The truck driver is sat on the rear step of an ambulance, a blanket wrapped around his shoulders and shaking from shock. He has the odd contusion but other than that looks okay. He keeps muttering that he couldn't stop the blow out, and something about not being able to help the lady. The paramedic is calming him and tells him that he called the emergency services quickly and that he couldn't have done more. He doesn't look like he believes her.

The grinding noise of metal being cut fills the air and along with it comes the smell of burning metal. They're obviously cutting her out. A stretcher with a backboard has been lowered down and it seems to take forever before we hear the shout 'She's out!". The timing is perfect as the helicopter has arrived and is landing a little further down the road, blowing dust up everywhere and making our eyes water. I pull my bandana up from around my neck and cover my nose and mouth. A medic runs over and quickly descends over the edge of the drop.

We all gather at the edge, ready to help pull up the ropes when we're asked and one of the medics turns to me and asks if I'll help carry the stretcher to the ambulance when it gets up. Apparently, there's a risk of the car exploding from a fuel leak, so the fire brigade is going to concentrate on sorting that out. It's been a dry summer and the woods down there are dry as anything. It would be like setting light to tinder if that car goes up.

The medics make slow progress up the hill, pausing frequently to adjust equipment and ensure their patient is still breathing. It feels like it takes forever, but in reality, can only have been moments. The first helmet appears over the drop off and is closely followed by two more. I rush forward to assist with the stretcher, taking the weight as it comes into view.

Whoever is on there is lucky to be alive, their facial features are obscured by blood pouring from a wound on the forehead. The chief medic moves to the head of the stretcher and indicates for me to move around the side. Once everyone is in place we move as quickly as we can towards the helicopter.

I feel something move and look down; there's a hand next to mine where I'm holding the stretcher. My heart drops when I recognize the bracelet around the wrist. It's exactly like the one I bought Sue for her birthday.

The stretcher is secured in the helicopter and its only when it's taken off that I rush back to the edge of the drop and look over. The car beneath is barely recognizable, but the door that's been cut off is visible, discarded to one side. All the way to the drop I prayed that I was wrong, that it would be a blue car, not a red car. The door lays there mocking me, scratched red paint on display.

I pull my phone from my jeans and hit the speed dial, praying that she'll pick up and tell me to fuck off. Over the sound of the bustle from the emergency services a ring tone is heard loud and clear. It's her phone. We'd joked about the ringtone she'd recently chosen for me. Warrant's Cherry Pie after we'd watched the male strippers from England perform a routine at the Severed MC clubhouse.

I drop to my knees, staring at my phone as the voicemail kicks in and I hear her voice.

It was Sue.

CHAPTER TWO

Jackson

The waiting room is packed with the guys from Hellion and Severed MC's. We're not Sue's legal family, even though she's family to us, so they won't let us in to see her but one of the nurses took sympathy on me and let me know that she's in surgery, but she's expected to be there for a long time. From the look on her face, it's not good news.

Rebel is sitting with Eve and Teresa, all of them looking absolutely shell shocked. We all are. Looking around the room I see all the family I don't think she realizes she has, all concerned for her, all loving her. I feel like even more of a shit now for breaking things off between us. I wish I could take it back. I wish the words had never been spoken. I wish she hadn't been on that road! It's too late for wishes now though.

The door to the waiting room opens and a guy I don't immediately recognize walks in. When he sees all the leather cuts he visibly blanches, I can see his whole body goes tense and he looks like he's seriously considering running. As he checks out the patches some of the tension eases from his shoulders and he moves over to one of the empty seats. When I look closer, I recognize him as the driver of the eighteen wheeler. Rushing over I pull him up with both hands using the collar of his shirt, my face practically touching his. He's crying for fucks sake, as far as I'm concerned this is all on him, it's all his fault. Rage fills me and I'm about to give him something to cry about, but I'm pulled off him as strong arms encircle me, forcing me back. It's Wrath. I throw him a disgusted look but still step back, not too far though, meaning the truck driver still looks intimidated by me.

"I'm sorry about your friend," his voice is gentle and weak. "I tried... I couldn't... I'm sorry." With that the shock takes over and he collapses back into the chair. Rebel pushes me aside calling me a lot of names, ass being the tamest, and drops to her knees in front of him. She talks softly, reassuring him.

"It's okay, we know it wasn't your fault." I grunt when she says that and am rewarded with one of her looks. The 'don't mess with me' look that I know too well, so I shut up and hover.

"The tire blew out, I wasn't speeding or anything, but I couldn't control the truck. I'm so sorry."

"Have the police spoken to you?" I snap.

He nods, "I gave them my statement, I couldn't do anything. I don't get it. I check my rig all the time. I keep my tires fresh; it shouldn't have happened." You can hear the confusion and disbelief in his voice. Part of me wants to understand, to comfort him, he's right, he probably didn't do anything wrong. The other part of me still sees Sue on that stretcher, unrecognizable. Right now, he's the only person that I can hold responsible, that I can blame. I want to take this guy outside and beat him into the seventh circle of hell. This is his fault.

"What are you doing here?" Anger seeps out with my words. Rebel snaps her head around at the harshness in my voice, but I ignore her.

"I needed to make sure she's okay," he almost whispers. "I feel so guilty."

"So you fucking should, she's probably going to die and it's all on you!" I scream out. The room goes silent, they're all staring at me and it's obvious they're startled by my loud outburst. Wrath moves in closer and places his hand on my shoulder.

"I believe him." Wrath is a man of few words, he used to be an enforcer for another MC till he lost someone close to him, someone close to all of us. He has a way of reading people, and I've never found him to be wrong. "There's more to this story though, this wasn't an accident."

The old guy looks up in horror when he hears Wrath's

words and there's an expression on his face I can't quite read.

"No, they couldn't. They wouldn't." He doesn't get any more words out as he breaks down sobbing. Rebel places her hand on his knee and tries to comfort him, but his tears are heartfelt.

It takes a good while for him to calm down, by which point I and several of my brothers have pulled up chairs to be close to him. We've formed a semi-circle in front of him and I'd be the first to admit it must be intimidating as hell to be surrounded by two MC's all wanting answers.

When he finally regains control of himself, I'm the first to talk.

"I think you need to tell us what you mean by that last statement. What's going on here?" My voice is still firm, but no longer as aggressive as it was.

Rebel turns and gives me another dirty look. "I think we need to do introductions first. I'm Rebel and this is my dad, Jackson. We're from Maldon. Sue, the lady in the car used to go out with my dad. She's family to us, and these guys," she indicates the guys from Severed, "are her other family from Severed."

I flinch when she uses the past tense, but she's right. I dumped Sue, I should have been there for her.

"I'm Bert," the old trucker replies. "I don't have a family anymore. I lost my wife Charlotte last year. We were never blessed with kids." I harrumph as I'm not interested in hearing his life story and am impatient for him to tell us what happened, but he puts up a hand to stall me. "It's relevant," he explains. "All I have is my truck. I like to keep busy, and I work for myself. About a month ago some guys approached me, wanting me to carry a cargo for them and I refused, they've been hassling me ever since to change my mind. I don't have any family for them to threaten, which is one of the reasons they picked me, if anything happened to me no one would come looking for me. They offered me a lot of money, too much money for it to be anything other than an illegal cargo but at my age and stage of life money doesn't matter. I've got my truck and that's all I need so it was easy to turn them down. They didn't like that."

I can't help myself; I can't sit still any longer, so I stand and start pacing the floor. "Why do you think it's them?"

"Because I answered no, a lot. There's no way I'm carrying that cargo for them. They told me that if I went to the police, they'd kill me, so I stayed quiet and kept my head down, but they kept hassling me. It can only be them, I can't figure it out, but they must have done something to my rig to cause that blow out."

"Who? Who are you talking about?" I snap.

"Carnal MC, they've been into all sorts of shady shit ever since their President got killed in that explosion last year and I want no part of it."

There's a collective gasp from the Severed guys when they hear the name of the rival MC that almost destroyed them.

17

Angel stands and punches the wall in anger. "Will this shit never end!" Eve tries to comfort him, but he pushes her away and starts pacing the room as well.

I nod at Bert to continue his story, watching Angel from the corner of my eye to make sure he's okay. I get it, Carnal MC almost wiped out everything he loved but I thought it had all been brought back under control now.

"Carnal have always dealt in guns and drugs and that's as far as the old President would let them go, but since he passed there's been a lot of infighting and they've decided to go into a more profitable trade, human trafficking."

"What the hell!" Rebel stands suddenly, and we're all just as shocked as she is.

"I can't do that. I can't knowingly transport those poor girls in my truck. I'd rather die first, that's what I told them. I think that's why they did what they did somehow, they caused that blow out and now your friend is hurt and it's all my fault." Bert wrings his hands in his lap.

"We're here, we'll help you!" Rebel exclaims, making promises on behalf of the rest of us that she can't possibly keep. I'm not sure about Severed but Hellion certainly isn't equipped to deal with an enemy the likes of Carnal. This is way out of our league.

"Darlin'," I try and appeal to her. "We can't go up against Carnal. We're not prepared for something like this."

Angel stands, "Alone we can't," he explains, "but I know a man. He helped us out last time we had a problem in

Severed. I'm sure if we asked, he'd come back. He's one of us now."

He's told me about what happened last year, and I agree, if anyone can help us he can.

Angel pulls out his phone and starts to leave the room, declaring "I'm calling Declan."

CHAPTER THREE

Jackson

As Angel leaves the room to call Declan a nurse comes in. She takes a sudden step back, a look of surprise on her face, when she sees just how many of us are in here waiting for news.

Several voices clamor over each other asking how Sue is but the nurse uses her hands to signal that we need to shut up and listen to her. It takes a few moments but eventually the room goes silent.

"Your friend is still in surgery, and I need to ask if any of you are O negative, she's lost a lot of blood due to her injuries and we're running low. I'm afraid that's the only type your friend can accept." She looks around the room quickly and is about to leave when both Rebel and Aaron stand and say "I am" at the same time.

"Oh," the nurse seems a little shocked. "That's good. I didn't expect to find two of you. Could you come with me please and we'll get you set up."

"Is there anything the rest of us can do to help?" I voice what I know the rest of the room is thinking.

"Well, if any of you would like to donate to help other patients we'll never say no, but we need to get this donation sorted as a priority." She turns to leave the room with Aaron and Rebel but pauses. "Your friend is a fighter; we didn't expect her to make it through this far. We'll let you know how she's doing as soon as we can." With that she's gone and the tension in the room is back.

I sit down in the chair nearest to me and put my head in my hands. I can't even help Sue by donating my blood. I'm AB positive so can only donate to another AB positive recipient. I feel so bloody useless. I sense someone sit in the chair beside me and turn when Smokey places her hand on my arm.

"You heard her, she's a fighter. We've got to believe she's going to be okay." Smokey reassures me in her gentle voice.

"I let her down," my voice breaks. "I should have been there for her, but instead I quit on us."

She looks as though she's about to say something else but is interrupted when Angel returns. He stands facing the room.

"I've spoken to Declan and he and his guys will be here tomorrow. He was coming home in a few days anyway, now that his grandmother's estate has been settled." There are relieved sighs around the room from the Severed cohort. I've not met Declan as he was away when we visited Severed to meet up with Eve's friends from England, but I've heard mention of him. He's not a part of the club, but he'd bought the local pub. He's ex-military and stepped up and offered to help when they were having problems with a drug cartel as he didn't want that on his doorstep any more than the Severed guys did. Angel always speaks about him with respect and that's good enough for me.

"What can Hellion do?" I stand, offering the help of my club. I'm not sure what use we'll be as we're all almost double the age of the guys from Severed, but what we lack in agility we make up for in experience. Most of us are ex-military ourselves.

Angel speaks, "We need to get as much intel together as we can for when Declan arrives." He looks around the room. "Ladies, can you go sort out some refreshments?" Teresa harrumphs at his request, but he gives her a look that asks her to comply. Eve doesn't even question it; she's already gathering their bags and sweaters.

Smokey comes over and tells me that while she's here she's going to go check in on James, he's one of our prospects who was badly hurt in a fire that destroyed her house recently and he's back in hospital receiving treatment for the side effect of his burns.

Once the women have left the room all eyes turn to Bert. He looks a little intimidated but, all credit to the guy, he stands his ground.

"What do you need to know?" He directs his question at Angel.

"I think you should start at the beginning, tell us everything, even if you don't think it's important. It might be something you think is insignificant that is the key to all this."

Bert nods and takes a moment to compose his thoughts. He's about to start speaking when Angel asks him if he's okay with him recording this so he can play it back to Declan when he gets here. Bert agrees and Angel starts the recording app on his phone.

"I guess it was about three months ago that I first noticed them, it was one of those things I just put down to coincidence. They seemed to be in the same truck stops as me when I was doing my run to the docks to pick up a load. You get used to seeing the same faces on the road, but these guys were new, and they stood out because they were bikers rather than truckers. I didn't really think anything of it at the time. It was only later, after they'd contacted me that I figured out they must have been watching me.

I do a run to the docks in Melbourne every couple of weeks and pick up a load then transport it to a warehouse for a motorcycle dealer in Bendigo. They collared me at the service center in Avenel. I often stop off there for breakfast on the way to the docks. The toilets are outside and they kind of ambushed me in there. They explained that they had a cargo they wanted delivering to the docks on the days that I did my pickups, and as I was already going there empty it was beneficial to both of us.

There was just something about these guys, they gave me the creeps, so I politely told them that I had enough work on and wasn't looking for any new clients. One of them pulled a knife on me and held it to my throat. He called me by my name which spooked me. He told me that he didn't care what I wanted, they had a load they needed delivering and I was going to deliver it... or else. Luckily someone wandered over to use the toilets and interrupted them and I was able to get away.

It happened again at the same services on my next journey and once again I replied no. I stopped dropping in there just in case. Shortly after that I started getting threatening notes at my home. They knew where I lived. I'm a widower and as we had no kids I decided to be a stubborn old coot and ignore them. I knew that whatever they wanted me to transport wouldn't be legal, but I guess in the back of my mind I just assumed it was drugs or guns or something like that.

I started varying my route, hoping to throw them off, I even started sleeping in the truck and not going home but it didn't help. They found me at a different truck stop last night. I woke up and they were in my cab with a gun to my head. I decided to let them think I was going to go along with their plan, and they started talking about building a hidden section in the back of the trailer. When I heard the dimensions I worked out that they must be planning on transporting people, not guns. Then one of the guys let something slip about the merchandise, calling it 'they' and that was enough for me.

They must have sensed I wasn't going to go through with it though. I'm not sure how they managed to cause the tire to blow out, but it must have been them. I take good care of my rig, it's my life. I know my tires were all in good condition."

Bert's shoulders sag as he finishes telling his story. I have so many questions but Angel's leading this, I'll wait till he's done.

"They could have punctured the tire sidewall," Cowboy offers. He's one of the Severed guys. "If they punctured it with a thin blade that would do it, you wouldn't have noticed when you set off, but it would have caused the cords to break down as you drove as they can't handle the extra load. It's called a zipper fracture." He explains.

"How the hell do you know all that?" Angel queries.

"I couldn't sleep and was watching one of those cheesy road crash lawyer ads on TV, it was all about trailer blow outs and I was so bored I looked it all up on their website." He admits.

"He's right," Bert offers. "If it was a thin enough blade I probably wouldn't have noticed. I do a visual check for nails and debris. The sidewall's the weakest part of the tire." Bert's head hangs low. "I'm so sorry, your friend getting hurt is all on me. I really didn't think they'd do anything like that."

"It's not your fault, you didn't know, and it was just bad timing you were both on that stretch of road when it happened. Another five minutes either way and you'd have both come out of it with nothing more than a few cuts and scrapes." Angel acknowledges. He's right.

Hard to think that fate is so fickle that my woman's life is in the balance for the sake of five minutes. I register that I still think of her as my woman. She needs to pull through this so I can fix it. I need to make her mine again.

CHAPTER FOUR

Rebel

Waiting for updates on Sue's condition is soul destroying, but at least by donating blood I feel like I'm doing something. The waiting room is a soulless place, it almost feels like it's deaths waiting room, you're just sat there in anticipation of the bad news that's to come.

I'm glad to hear she's a fighter. I know that deep down Jackson loves her, he's just too stupid and too scared to admit it. I can't remember him bringing anyone back to the house when I was growing up, but I'm not naive enough to believe he didn't have female companions. As I grew older I understood that he was doing it to protect me, but when I tried to talk to him about it when I was leaving for university he would just shut me down. I don't want him to spend his life alone, I never did, although I admit that as a child I could be selfish about him spending all his spare time with me. I've been told stories of the odd tantrum or two I'd thrown when I suspected he had a date.

Aaron is silent as we follow the nurse down the sterile corridor but when he notices me looking at him he pulls me into a hug. "She's going to be okay," he reassures me. "They're both going to be okay."

Aaron and Jackson have been best friends since they were in the military together, and both gravitated to Hellion MC when they left. I know they both saw active service and share some nightmare memories, but thanks to the Club they're in a good place. That sense of belonging and brotherhood was important to them, and let's face it, if it wasn't for the Club who knows where I'd be now after being abandoned at their gates as a baby.

It's unbelievable that I now have a relationship with my mom, and that I almost lost her as soon as I'd found her thanks to her abusive asshole of a husband. I'm very grateful to have her in my life now. My upbringing may have been anything but conventional, a baby girl being adopted by a bunch of tattooed bikers, but I can't imagine having a more caring, loving and supportive environment to grow up in. It's why I opened the Double D ranch, I wanted to give abandoned and needy children hope, show them that there is a better future out there for them. I know Jackson is really pleased that I used the land he signed over to me for such a good cause, especially when that same land almost destroyed everything we knew. It was a rough time for us all, and sadly we lost one of our prospects, Harry, as a result.

A few months ago, we also lost Bandit, one of the original MC founders. Cancer sucks big time. But as a Club we're there for his widow Smokey and thankfully it's brought Wrath back into her life. They became his guardians when he lost his own mother to cancer as a teenager. James, our prospect, is upstairs on a ward receiving treatment as a result of some horrific burns he suffered when he tried to rescue Bandit from the house when it went up in flames. He didn't know Bandit was already gone and rushed in to save him, no thought of his own safety. The Club has made sure he's always got visitors, even on days when he's so depressed he doesn't want them. He doesn't know it yet but as soon as he's fully recovered he's being patched in. His bravery has ensured he'll have a place with Hellion for life. I just hope that he has some quality of life when he gets out of here. The docs seem to think with time he'll be fine. Here's hoping.

The phlebotomy suite is clean and sterile when we enter. A nurse comes over and greets us both whilst the nurse who accompanied us lets her know what we're here for.

We're shown to large comfortable chairs, and the phlebotomy nurse explains what's going to happen.

"We need to take a sample of blood first that we can send to the lab, just to confirm that you are O negative. I'm not sure if you know but an O negative recipient can only accept blood from an O negative donor, yet they can donate to anyone. Bit of a cruel twist."

"I never knew that, guess I've been lucky that I never

needed it myself." I answer. I hadn't quite understood how complex this all was.

Aaron has remained quiet throughout and he looks like he's lost in thought. Maybe the big guy doesn't like needles. It's not unheard of. I hope he's not going to pass out on me!

The phlebotomy nurse places a tourniquet around my arm and draws a syringe full of blood, then replaces the tube so that the donation bag is now being filled.

"This shouldn't take too long," she offers, "then after that I'm sure we can find you a cup of tea and a biscuit." She smiles at me before moving over and repeating the same procedure on Aaron. He's still not speaking and just looking straight ahead. I'd reach out and comfort him, but the chairs are set slightly too far apart.

"Are you okay?" I whisper loudly in his direction. Despite trying to be discreet the nurse still hears me and smiles over at us from the counter she's working at.

"Yeah, just thinking." From the expression on his face, he's thinking about something pretty serious.

"What about?" I'm curious now as this isn't how Aaron normally reacts to a situation.

"Nurse, can I ask you a question?" Aaron directs his query over to the nurse at the counter.

"Sure, what's up?" She moves back over to stand beside him.

"I remember back in the day the Army telling us all about blood types on some basic medical field training, but it's a little fuzzy now. Can an AB father have an O negative child?"

I look at him in confusion as I've no idea where he's going with this.

"No, an AB father would have a child with A, B or AB," the nurse confirms. Aaron thanks her and she goes back to what she was doing, meanwhile the blood bags fill slowly at either side of us.

"What's that all about?" I question Aaron. He's piqued my interest now, is he querying his heritage?

"Nothing, just idle curiosity, "he responds then promptly changes the subject. "So why did Jackson break up with Sue?" I knew it, these bikers are just as bad as old women for gossip!

"I think he got scared," I admit. "He's never had anyone serious before and I think that he was starting to feel that way about Sue and it kind of freaked him out."

"He did have someone," Aaron shocks me with his statement. "Back when you were little. You were too young to understand really, but you could tell something was off as you were really clingy with him. It's not my story to tell, but he let her go because he loved you more."

I take in a deep breath of air, how did I not know this, and why is Aaron telling me now? Will it do any good raking up the past other than to make me feel guilty as hell?

"But, why? I only ever wanted him to be happy." I protest.

"I think he got scared, felt he had to make a choice and, without wanting to sound harsh, you were the safe option." Aaron admits.

"I wish he hadn't." I sigh. "I've only ever wanted Jackson to be happy."

"You know we all love you, and we all wanted to keep you, but it's Jackson who fought for you. Deep down we all thought he was your biological Dad, but he never wanted to know for certain, and when you were old enough to choose you didn't want to know either."

"No, he's my dad in every way that counts. He's the one that raised me, he's the one who held me when I cried. Anyone else is just a sperm donor. I know you all stepped in, and I love you all, but he's the one I've always thought of as my dad." This is a bloody deep conversation for this time of night and it's making me uncomfortable.

"Why are you bringing this up now? Why tonight?" I question.

"Because I always believed he was your dad, until tonight."

"I'm confused, where are you going with this? What changed tonight?"

"Jackson has AB blood, Rebel. He can't be your father." He states calmly. His next words floor me.

"I think I am!"

CHAPTER FIVE

Rebel

"What the fuck!" I screech loudly, startling the nurse who's doing her best to stay away from this conversation, bless her. "Why tell me now! I don't believe you."

Aaron looks bereft. I guess my reaction isn't quite what he expected when he told me he thought he was my father, rather than Jackson.

"I always thought Jackson was your dad," he admits, his voice soft. "Back then Jackson partied harder than me. I was still wary of strangers. I'm not saying he slept around, but he lived his life to the full whilst I kind of holed up in my room most of the time." He turns to the nurse and asks if he can have a glass of water then waits until he has it before he continues. Meanwhile the nurse is now watching, fascinated. I can see why, it's like the plot of a Hallmark movie unfolding in front of her.

"When Dee Dee showed up at your birthday party I recognized her, even after all those years. I'd slept with her that summer, only the once, and then she moved onto Jackson. I guess I wasn't rebellious enough for her," he chuckles. "Even back then, I was convinced Jackson was your dad."

"What changed?" I snap out. I can't help the bitterness in my tone. Everything I thought I knew has just been thrown into chaos.

"I never knew your blood type. It's not something that comes up in general conversation."

"So, you're telling me that you're basing all this on a blood type? What a load of baloney," I mutter.

"Erm…" the nurse moves closer, hesitating to interrupt our conversation. "He's right, honey. An AB blood type couldn't be your father, but another O negative could," she confirms.

"But I don't even look like you!" I protest.

"No, you look like your mom," Aaron tells me. "I see her in you every day."

My mind is in turmoil. It was bad enough my mom suddenly appearing in my life and turning it upside down, but now to tell me that Jackson isn't my dad has trumped that.

"What do you want? A medal?" I snap angrily.

"I'm sorry. I shouldn't have mentioned anything," Aaron apologizes. "I don't want Jackson to stop being your dad.

He's done an amazing job raising you, and in every sense of the word he's your father. Like you said, I'm just a donor." He looks so sad when he tells me he's just my donor.

Why am I being such a bitch? I know Aaron, I love Aaron. He's one of my dad's, and he always has been. I've always thought of the all the older guys at the MC as my dad's, I used to think I was really lucky compared to my friends at school as I had Dads plural whilst they only had the one. I think this has come as much of a shock to him as it has me, then a thought hits me.

"So, we know that Jackson can't be my dad. It doesn't mean that you are though?" I confront him.

"True, it's just a possibility. It's up to you if you want to find out." He runs his free hand through his hair in frustration. "I should have stayed quiet. I'm sorry." His repeated apologies are annoying me. I feel irrationally angry.

I'm feeling lightheaded and I'm not sure if it's because I'm donating blood, or just the shock of everything that's happening around me right now. What the hell has happened to my life since I hit thirty? My Mom suddenly turned up, we lost some good people as a result and nearly lost her. I almost got killed, then Bandit got cancer and died, and James got hurt. Now, Sue's upstairs fighting for her life and I'm sat here trying to comprehend what Aaron's telling me.

"I can't process this. It's too much, I can't…" with that I break into tears. That's not like me at all, I'm normally so strong. I'm more likely to shout before I cry. The nurse rushes over and puts her arm around my shoulder to comfort me as Aaron is still stuck in his chair until his donation bag is full.

"You've had a hell of an evening," she comforts me, "and I'm guessing you haven't eaten either?" I nod my head in confirmation. We were going to eat when Jackson got to mine, instead I'd received his panicked call to meet him here at the hospital. She looks down at my donation bag and nods in satisfaction when she sees it's now full. "Let's get you off this and down to the canteen, you need to get something to eat."

Yeah, right. Eating is the last thing on my mind right now and I'm not hungry. If anything, I feel sick. Aaron looks at me and I remember that this guy knows me inside out.

"She's right. You're no good to anyone if you get ill. Let's get you downstairs and get you some food." The nurse finishes unhooking him as well and he comes over to my chair. Resting on the seat arm he puts his arm around me and pulls me into a hug. It's not the first time I've cried on his shoulder, and I'm sure it won't be the last.

"I don't want a new Dad," I sob into his shoulder, big fat tears falling from my eyes.

"You haven't lost your old Dad," he comforts me. "You just got lucky and have a maybe extra Dad if you want him."

"I can't..." the words won't come out as I can't stop crying. I'm becoming hysterical. Aaron sits there soothing me, hushing me and rubbing his hand in small comforting strokes up and down my back.

When I finally come to my senses I notice that we're now alone in the room. The nurse has left to either give us some privacy or to take the blood to the operating theatre. I don't really care which, I'm just grateful there's no audience to my melt down.

"Do you think you can come and eat something?" Aaron's voice is full of concern.

"I'm not hungry, I feel sick." I complain.

"You need to eat something; do you think you could maybe manage a blueberry muffin?" Aaron knows me so well.

"No, but I could probably pick at one and move it around on the plate to make you think I was eating." I admit.

Aaron lets out a loud guffaw, sharing the same memory as me. The mealtimes when he'd be the one sitting with me making sure I ate my vegetables. I thought that if I moved them around enough on my plate he wouldn't notice that I wasn't actually eating them. I never won. If Aaron sat with me at lunch there was no escape, and my plate was always empty when it went back to the kitchen. He'd sit there for as long as it took to make sure I ate all my peas and carrots. He was the guy who taught me to eat them first, get the stuff I didn't like off my plate so I could enjoy what was left. This man won't hurt me. I know that. He's always had my back, always looked out for me.

I stand slowly and he wraps me in a huge bear hug. "We can keep this between us if you'd rather," he offers. "Whatever you want, darlin'."

"I need time," I admit. I feel safe here in his arms. I wish I could turn back the clock just one day, but I can't. What's done is done, what's said is said. It can't be taken back. The knowledge is out there now. It's up to me to decide what I do with it, how I handle it, without breaking this man's heart.

CHAPTER SIX

Jackson

E ve and Teresa return with coffees and teas from the canteen downstairs, I'm not sure where they found it, but they've commandeered one of the hostess trolleys the ward auxiliaries use to transport it. There's also a huge pile of muffins and cakes which are wolfed down in seconds by this lot. I'm not hungry. I'm too worried about Sue to eat right now.

Rebel and Aaron aren't back yet, and I'm aware that I've lost track of time. That's the thing with hospital waiting rooms, there's no sense of time and nothing to distract you. It could have been half an hour or only ten minutes. I sink back into my chair and put my head in my hands wondering how the hell Sue got caught up in this mess. Logic tells me it was just bad timing, but without that bad timing Bert wouldn't have come across all of us. Right now, we're probably the only hope he has.

I want to warm to the guy, he seems a decent bloke and he's genuinely cut up about what happened, but I can't help blaming him for the accident. Even knowing it's not his fault my anger still needs to be directed somewhere and right now he's the target.

I'm not an innocent but even I'm shocked to think that something like human trafficking is happening practically on my doorstep. We've come so far in terms of technology and medical advancements but seem to be regressing in terms of brutality and treating people as commodities. I shudder when I think what it would be like to lose Rebel to something as horrific as that.

I know that most trafficking in Australia is into the country, workers from Far East countries are lured here with false promises of employment then turned into modern day slaves when they arrive. They're promised a better lifestyle here and the ability to earn enough money to send home to support their poverty-stricken families. It's despicable. It sounds like Carnal have taken a different approach and are shipping girls out of the country. I guess it's a more profitable trade. I'd never have thought they were organized enough to pull off something like this. I've heard of them here and there over the years, but we've always stayed well away although Angel has told me how close Severed came to being destroyed by them. They were inexorably linked thanks to his twin brother, Satan who used to be Carnal's VP.

All heads turn when the door opens and a nurse I know

from the ranch, Cathy, comes in. She walks straight over to me.

"She's going to be okay; she's come through the surgery, and they've stopped the bleeding, but she's got a long recovery ahead of her." I breathe out a sigh of relief and wipe away moisture from my eyes with the back of my hand. "I know you're not technically next of kin but if anyone asks you're her fiancé," she tells me. I simply nod my head in agreement. Cathy helps out at the ranch when she can, she was brought up in the system and likes to give something back to the kids who are stuck in it now. "Do you want to sit with her?"

"Yeah, of course. Thanks, Cathy." She looks at the state of me and pulls me into a hug. I let her.

"She's going to be okay, Jackson. She was lucky." There are choruses of well wishes from the rest of the room as Cathy leads me away.

The walk to the ICU is quiet, neither of us feeling the need for words. When we get there the noise all comes from machines whooshing, beeping and such. It's strange, there's none of the bustle of a regular ward, no chatter. I can hear nurses talking gently to their comatose patients, explaining what they're doing and talking to them as though they were awake, but it's muted. There's a sense of quiet efficiency and, surprisingly, considering where we are, calm.

Before we go into the room that Sue is in, Cathy holds me back by my arm for a moment. "She's going to look worse than she actually is. The machines are breathing for her as we've kept her sedated, it's what her body needs to heal. There are a lot of machines, and it can look pretty intimidating," she reminds me. I silently nod my understanding, afraid to disturb this peaceful ambience with words.

Even though Cathy warned me, it's still a shock when I see Sue lying there. She looks so fragile, and smaller than I remember but that could be just because she's surrounded by machines. Cathy indicates a chair at the side of the bed for me and I take it, reaching hesitantly for Sue's hand, but looking to Cathy for permission to do so. She smiles.

"You can hold her hand, and talk to her, let her know you're here for her. Just don't get in the way of the wires or the machines. I'll be back in a bit." Cathy retreats silently, leaving me alone with Sue.

I rest my head on top of my hands where they're holding Sue's hand. "I'm sorry," I whisper. "I was a bloody stupid old fool, I should never have said what I did." I know that now. I should never have let Sue go. She's the best thing that's happened to me in a hell of a long time and I'd be stupid not to grab hold of that and make the most of it.

"I know I've never spoken the words out loud, but I love you," I confess. "I should have told you every day, should have shouted it from the rooftops." I pause, wondering if this is what I should be telling her right now, if she can even hear me, then think that if I can't say it now, when can I?

"You make my days brighter, darlin' and you make my heart race. I look forward to seeing you and being with you. I was just too dense to see that you're it for me. I let my stupid fear get in the way of you and me. I hope you'll forgive me."

Sue just lays there, her chest moving up and down in time with the respirator. Her eyes closed, her skin covered in blood and cuts and grazes. I can see the stitches on her forehead from the gash I'd seen at the crash site. My Sue would be sat up shouting and cursing at me, her fighting spirit taking me on. I just hope that she's fighting inside. Cathy seemed pretty certain that she's going to pull through. Right now, I'd love nothing more than to hear her calling me every name under the sun. I need her to wake up so I can put things right.

CHAPTER SEVEN

Rebel

As I suspected, I do nothing but pick at the blueberry muffin that Aaron bought for me, it's a mess of crumbs now on the plate.

The whole parent thing is hovering like an elephant in the room so rather than face it I decide to interrogate Aaron about something else he mentioned in the phlebotomy room.

"Tell me more about this woman that Jackson gave up for me when I was little."

"It's not my story to tell, Rebel. You should really talk about that with Jackson." Aaron tries to shut me down but I'm not having it.

"I think after the bombshell you've just thrown at me it's the least you can do. It's not like Jackson's going to be in a good place to talk for a while," I cajole. It works. Aaron looks uncomfortable but I think I'm breaking him down.

"When you were about four or so, Jackson met someone," Aaron starts.

"But he never brought anyone home?" I interrupt.

"No, that was his way. He didn't want to bring anyone home and confuse you, so he always met her away from the compound. Don't you remember our sleepovers?" A grin crosses his face at the memory.

"Yeah, they were fun," I admit. Sometimes Jackson would go away on business, or so he'd told me, and that meant I got to have a sleepover with Aaron. We'd make a tent out of bed sheets and chairs, throw blankets and pillows on the ground and lay there, Aaron telling me fantastic made-up stories about a princess who didn't need a prince, she used to fix everything herself. He'd twist the fairy tales so that no dashing prince ever came to the rescue, nor was he needed. Sleeping Beauty escaped from the tower herself, Snow White was too wise to eat the apple and lived happily ever after with the dwarves, but my favorite was Scheherazade who used her stories to beguile the monarch into not killing her.

"Well, some of those were nights when he was with her," he admits.

"What was she called?" I'm curious about the woman who obviously once held Jackson's heart.

"He called her Rose. I think that was a pet name though, not sure what her real name was."

"What happened?"

"Well as far as I know he got cold feet. She wanted to spend more time with him, and she also wanted to meet you, after all you were such a huge part of his life. I think that's what finished it off to be honest. He was always so protective of you, and like I told you, you must have known something was going on because you'd become really clingy with him. He chose you over her. Rose didn't take it so well and moved away. Last we heard, she was killed a couple of years later in a car wreck. I often thought they'd have got back together if she hadn't died."

I feel terrible, but what Aaron says sounds plausible. I remember I never wanted to share Jackson when I was younger and can acknowledge that I probably would have been a bitch if he'd brought a woman home to meet me. I was definitely a strong-willed child. The guys never fail to remind me of the many tantrums I threw when I was younger, mind you, I can still throw a good tantrum even now.

"What about you? I never see you with women," I pause. "You're not gay are you!" I suddenly blurt out, putting various things together. My voice was a little too loud on that last comment and the couple of heads in the canteen turn to see what the commotion is.

Aaron pales and for a moment I wonder if I'm right. "It's okay if you are, it's nothing to be ashamed of," I rush out.

"I just never met the right woman is all," he blurts out. "I've had a few long-term relationships but no one I ever wanted to make it last with."

Now I feel sorry for him and Jackson. Everyone should have someone. I think of my someone, Chris, and remember I haven't told him what's happened or where I am. He knew Jackson was coming over tonight for me to interrogate so Chris went to Melbourne to visit an old friend overnight. He'd not wanted to be in the way, and he isn't really on my side on this one. He thinks I should leave Jackson be and let him live his own life.

Moving in with someone means you give up a part of yourself, it's no longer just about you, and every day you make compromises for the other person. It's a partnership. It's not always an easy decision to make. I can see how someone like Jackson would balk at that commitment. What he doesn't see though is the upside of living with someone you love. For everything you give up, you get so much more in return. Don't get me wrong, not every day is plain sailing, and because we're both strong characters we often have blazing rows, but the makeup sex is out of this world and worth it.

Chris really likes Jackson and respects him; he had such a lousy upbringing himself he never fails to remind me how lucky I am to have had Jackson and my other Dads on my side. If it wasn't for them I'd have ended up in the system and be like the kids we help out at the ranch.

"So how are we going to handle this?" Aaron asks me.

"Can we keep it between us for now?" I hate the look of sorrow that flits across his face.

"Yeah, Jackson's got enough on his plate right now. It won't do any good to tell him about any of this."

"I need time as well," I admit. "I don't know if I want to know. I don't know that I need to know. Does that make sense?" I plead.

"Yeah, I guess it does. It's been a bit of a shock to me as well. Until tonight I always thought you were his. A part of me hopes you are mine; I love you and am so bloody proud of you, but if you're not I'm still glad to be part of your life." His words warm my heart but make me feel guilty.

What am I supposed to do? Do I want to know? Does it really make any difference now, all these years later. What will it change for the better if anything? This must be just as confusing for him as it is me.

"So, how about you eat some of that muffin instead of just playing with it?" Aaron's laugh when he finishes speaking brings a smile to my face.

I tilt my head coyly in response. "I'll think about it." I swirl the crumbs around the plate a little more, pretending. When I do try and eat them it proves impossible, I've made too much of a mess of it.

"Another coffee and a fresh muffin?" Aaron offers.

"Yeah, sounds like a plan." No sooner are the words out of

my mouth than my stomach starts gurgling loudly, protesting at the lack of food.

"Your stomach is singing to me! I'm flattered." Aaron always used to say that to me when I was little, and my tummy rumbled.

"I'm bloody embarrassed," I confess. "That was loud enough to wake the dead." I stop suddenly, remembering where we are and thinking that was a pretty insensitive comment considering.

"Well, I'd best get you that muffin then," Aaron stands and puts the dirty dishes on the tray to take back to the counter. "Sounded like your stomach was out of tune just now." He leaves me with a cheeky wink as he heads back to the counter.

CHAPTER EIGHT

Rebel

When I return to the waiting room Jackson's not there. I'm relieved in a way as it means I don't have to put on a face for him. He'll know something's wrong and now isn't the time for this conversation. He needs to concentrate on Sue. I'm delighted when they tell me that she's out of surgery and Jackson is sitting with her.

I'm restless and nervy and can't settle. I keep sneaking glances at Aaron and catch him watching me as I pace.

"Why don't you go check on Smokey?" Aaron suggests, picking up on my mood and knowing I need a distraction. "She's gone up to see James."

I didn't think they'd let James have visitors this late in the hospital, but I head up to the floor where his room is anyway. He's had to come back several times since he was first released as he keeps getting infections in the burn sites and has to be admitted and put on an IV drip.

He's lucky, he'll recover from his burns eventually, but he has a long couple of years ahead of him before all the scars heal. I know Smokey worries more about his mental health now, he won't talk about what happened that day. At least he follows the doctors' advice and is constantly putting on lotion and drinking plenty of water, but we both think he needs to rest more and let his body heal. Wrath has been working with him in the gym to make sure he does the exercises he needs to do, in order to make sure the scars stretch as they heal and grow.

I think he spends too much time in the gym, it's an easy way of blocking things out. When you're in the gym you have to concentrate on what you're doing, the equipment you're using so there's no room for thoughts that would send you mad. Wrath's a man of few words so I'm pretty certain they're not talking through James's problems in there.

Smokey has taken him under her wing, she feels responsible for him. As she sees it, it's her fault the fire started and James was just trying to save her husband, Bandit. He didn't know he was already dead.

When you look back over this last eighteen months it's been truly crazy, whatever happened to our normal peaceful steady way of life. I kind of feel like I've stepped into the plot of a bad disaster movie. Every time it looks like things might be settling down again for us, something else happens.

The elevator doors open onto a dimly lit corridor. Aside from the odd beep of a machine it's quiet here. I'm grateful I have my Vans on and not my heels as I move along the tiled floor. The nurse on reception looks up and gives me a smile of greeting as she recognizes me. We spent many hours here when James was first admitted.

"Room 7," she whispers. "Smokey's in with him but you can join her if you promise not to wake him up."

"Thanks," I acknowledge her, equally as quietly.

I'm pleased to see that James is fast asleep and looks peaceful. Smokey is sitting in the chair beside the bed just sat quietly watching him. She looks a little surprised to see me but gives me a warm smile in greeting and points to the chair beside her which I take.

"Any news?" Her voice is soft and low, and I have to strain to hear the words, she obviously doesn't want to disturb James.

"She's out of surgery and in ICU," I pause. "Jackson's with her."

Smokey nods her head and a smile flits across her face. "She's strong, she'll be fine."

I wish I had Smokey's optimism, I just hope she's right.

I sit there and the silence doesn't bring me the peace I'd hoped for, instead my mind is going at a hundred miles per hour trying to process what I've learned tonight. Do I want to know? Do I need to know? But there's not just me to consider now, I'm guessing that Aaron wants to know.

Would it be selfish of me not to do the test and give him that closure.

What if he is my dad? What happens then? Surely ignorance and sweeping it back under the carpet is best for everyone? It would be best for me and Jackson, but deep down I know that wouldn't be right, Aaron deserves to know for sure.

Smokey can tell that something isn't right with me and calls me out on it. "What's wrong, Rebel? You look like you have a whole mess of busy going on in that head of yours?"

"I'm fine," I lie. "Guess I'm just worried about Sue, and James here." I try and deflect her attention to the bed before us.

"Really?" Smokey cocks her head and gives me a deeper inspection. "Feels like it's more than that. Is everything okay between you and Chris?"

Shit! As soon as she mentions Chris's name I realize I haven't told him what's happened. I look at my watch and see how stupidly early it is in the morning. I can't ring him now, he'll either still be out partying with his friend or he'll be crashed out.

"It's good, thanks. He's out partying with an old friend tonight so I didn't want to bother him until we knew what was happening. Guess I left it a little late."

"He'd want to know, Rebel. He'd want to be here for you, to support you. That's what couples do." Her words are softly spoken so as not to disturb James, but I can still hear the pain in her voice. She misses Bandit so much. They were together for over forty years, bless them.

"Come on, let's get you home. It's been a long night, and this guy looks like he's going to be fine." You can hear the affection in Smokey's voice when she talks about James. I glance across at him and it seems like the IV is working, he looks peaceful. I know Smokey wouldn't have left him if he was showing any sign of distress or restlessness.

Rising from the chair everything aches, I've spent too long this evening in uncomfortable hospital chairs. What I wouldn't give right now for one of Chris's back rubs. Once we're back on the ground floor I text Chris and ask him to call me when he wakes up, I don't tell him about the accident as I don't want to alarm him.

Smokey heads into the waiting room and takes charge.

"Right, you lot, she's out of surgery and Jackson's with her so there's nothing more any of us can do this evening. Go home, get some sleep, grab a shower and we can regroup in the morning."

I laugh at this lovely old lady telling a room full of bikers what to do, but they do as they're told without complaint. That's how much respect they have for her.

Our clubhouse isn't as posh as the one over in Severed so we agree that the Severed guys will stay in our homes instead. It's the least we can do under the circumstances. Angel and Eve come with me, Prez and Teresa head off with Smokey and Aaron takes the stragglers.

Aaron's obviously been catching up in my absence and addresses the room. "Meeting in our Church at ten am, that okay with you guys?" The guys all voice their agreement. What macho bullshit are they pulling now? I'm even more surprised when Aaron invites Bert to the meeting. What the hell's going on here? One thing for sure, as a woman I'll be the last one to know.

CHAPTER NINE

Jackson

It's still early when I'm woken by the nurse coming in to check Sue's vitals, she apologizes for disturbing me. I've fallen asleep leaning over the bed, my hand still holding hers. I panic for a moment thinking I may have caught one of the cables or tubes but it's fine, which is more than I can say for my neck right now. It hurts like hell having been cricked in that position, even if it was only for a few hours.

The nurse persuades me to go grab a few minutes of fresh air and a coffee as she'll be there for a while, and I gladly accept. She'd tried to persuade me to go home, but that's not going to happen any time soon. I need to make sure I'm here for her when she wakes, I'm just so bloody grateful that I'm going to get this second chance with her. I've been such a goddamn fool. When I declared I was leaving I also told her I was doing it for her, whereas in reality, I was just trying to save my heart from getting broken again.

At my age I should know better than to let the fear of what might never happen control me. Sure, Sue might leave me, but I'd rather spend time with her until that happens, if it happens. When I saw the wreck of her car last night I knew I couldn't let her go, no matter the cost in the future. It's not fair to judge Sue based on what's happened in the past. Not only are they different people, but it's also a different time and place altogether.

It's still very early morning so there's barely any traffic outside. With the slight chill in the air and the lack of noise I find myself relaxing on a bench under some trees with a coffee. It's tranquil here. I can't help wondering how many people have sat here before me, having received the worst news of their lives or perhaps the best. Looking across at the hospital I have to remind myself that this is a place of good as well. Every life that's lost is replaced by a new life, for every terminal diagnosis someone else gets the all clear. On the ward, amidst all the machines, it's too easy to forget the good things that happen here as well.

I'm in awe of the staff who work here, I really don't know how they can do it day after day and still retain their compassion and calm. I've mentioned it to Cathy before when she's been helping at the ranch, but she just shrugs it off as it's all just part of her job. There's something deep inside these people who choose to do this for a living, and it's something incredibly special.

I try and hold my head back for a moment, then roll my shoulders and crick my neck side to side to try and ease off the aches and kinks.

"Is this seat taken?" I was so lost in my thoughts that I failed to see the old lady approach the bench. She stands in front of me, a coffee in her hand and the tracks of tears stain her face. I stand immediately and offer her a seat next to me; my Mamma would whup my ass if I didn't stand for a lady. "Thank you." Her voice is quiet and gentle as she sits. I wonder what her story is.

She grimaces as she takes a sip of the bitter coffee, I recognize the vending machine cup and know how dreadful it tastes so offer her a look of sympathy. "It's certainly not a Costa is it?" I smile at her.

"You can say that again, still, it's better than nothing," she pauses and grimaces at the cup again, "well, maybe not." It's not a laugh but her face does have a smile as she speaks the last few words.

I'm not sure what the etiquette is here, should I talk to her? Leave her alone? I don't want to appear rude, but neither do I want to intrude so I sit there feeling awkward in my silence. I try not to stare but it's hard to miss the tear tracks on her face and I find myself glancing over at her as I sip at my own disappointing coffee. Eventually I can't resist.

"Are you okay? You look like you've been crying?" Talk about stating the bloody obvious.

"Oh, bless you, I'm fine, thank you for asking though." She moves her hand on top of mine and pats it softly. "I've actually had one of the best nights of my life." Her smile lights up her whole face, it's full of love and pride. "I've just met my great grandson, and they've named him after my late husband, Arthur. It's a day I thought I'd never live to see." A lone tear falls again, and I hand her a tissue. I'm not sure how I ended up with a pocket pack of tissues, it's not something I'd normally have on me, but I vaguely recall Rebel handing them to me to keep safe for her in the waiting room.

"That's pretty awesome," I agree.

"It is, isn't it? I just wish Arthur could have been here to see his name sake; he'd have been so proud." She fumbles around in her bag for a moment and pulls out a phone. When she's found the photo she was looking for she hands the phone to me. All I see is a scrunched-up baby face mid bawl, but I tell her what a grand looking baby she has, knowing that's what she needs to hear.

"Do you have children?" I notice the slight pause when she tries to gauge my age and choose between children and grandchildren.

"Not of my own," I admit sadly. "But I do have the most awesome adopted daughter." Just thinking of Rebel makes my heart swell with pride and I find myself pulling out my phone and sharing photos as well.

"Oh, she's beautiful," my companion praises, I can hear the warmth in her voice so know she's not just saying it to be polite. "Is she the reason you're here?"

"No, my partner had a really bad car accident last night so I'm here for her." I quickly check my watch to see how long I've been out here, but it's not as long as I thought.

"I'm sorry to hear that," she hesitates a moment, "is she going to be okay?"

"She will be," I reassure her. "She's got a rough few weeks ahead of her, but she'll be fine in the long run." If I say it often enough I'm hoping it will be true.

"Where are my manners!" She exclaims, "I should introduce myself; I'm Edith." She holds her hand out for me to shake.

"Mine too!" I apologize. "I'm pleased to meet you Edith, I'm Jackson."

We engage in small talk for a few more minutes before I apologize that I have to get back to the room and check on Sue. It's been a bit of light relief sat here chatting to Edith, who is an absolute treasure to talk to.

"It's been a pleasure, young man." She reaches over and gives me a warm hug. "I'll probably be visiting Arthur again before he goes home, so if you see me sat here please do come and join me."

I thank Edith and assure her that I will take her up on her kind offer. I have to say that's one of the most surreal coffee moments I've had, but there's something incredibly calming about the time I've spent chatting to her. I call into the waiting room on my way back, not expecting anyone to still be here, but it's full of people who care about Sue. I give them a quick update and let them know they should get home; they won't be allowed to visit with her while she's still sedated, and I promise to give them regular updates.

I return to Sue's room with a slightly lighter step than when I came out. It's time to go check on my woman. I can't wait for her to wake up so I can let her know what an idiot I've been.

CHAPTER TEN

Jackson

It doesn't feel right leaving Sue's bedside, but Aaron messaged me about the meeting in Church, saying he wants me there. Rebel is sitting with Sue until I can get back so at least she's not alone and Cathy assured me that Sue won't be waking up any time soon. Her body needs to heal before they'll consider bringing her round.

Our Church has never seemed so full, as well as the guys from Severed and Bert there are a couple of guys I've not seen before. Angel introduces them as Declan and Cam, they're some of the ex-military guys he was telling us about last night. I wasn't expecting to see them so soon, but Declan explains they have a friend in high places who occasionally lets them have access to his private jet as well as some high-tech toys when needed.

Aaron calls the meeting to order and gives everyone a brief summary of what's happened so far. Angel introduces

Declan and Cam to the room and asks Declan for his own update.

"I rang my contact straight after you called me last night and let him know what's going on. He's given me access to everything we might need," Declan starts. "For those of you who don't know us, Cam and I are ex-military and along with some of my old team we helped Prez and Angel sort out a drug issue over in Severed a while ago with a bit of help from another member of my old team. I don't know quite who he works for, but he's part of some privately funded setup that has access to shitloads of the latest tech and seems to work off the books for the government on occasion when they can't be seen to be involved. I get the impression it's an 'ask no questions' set up.

I sent him the recording you guys made last night, and the early feedback is that they're not aware of a trafficking set up in the area, but that could just be because they haven't got it up and running yet. There's been no noise on the subject yet, however, it doesn't mean it isn't happening or about to happen and they're keen to ensure it doesn't." Declan pauses for a moment, and I can see that he looks uncomfortable with what he's about to say.

"They've asked us not to get in the way, they want this set up to go ahead so they can find out who's funding it and where the girls are going." He's interrupted by a chorus of shouts and hell no's from around the table.

Aaron calms the room down eventually and apologizes to Declan, letting him know that he can continue.

"I know, this goes against everything that I believe in as well. It doesn't sit right with me, but I kind of get their point. If we stop it now, they'll just find another route out of the country, it won't stop it happening, and we'll have no idea when or where.

What they're asking is for us to work with Bert and let them think they've scared him into working for them, but we'll be there in the background, watching and learning all the way. They'll supply us with some tech we can fit to the trailer that won't be detectable and will allow us to track it wherever it goes. The girls won't be leaving the country, I promise you that. Between us we can ensure that there's always someone there, in the background so Bert is safe."

Declan looks over to Bert for his reaction. This is a huge ask of him, and he's not used to being involved in something like this.

"It makes me sick to my stomach to think that I'd be a party to what's happening to those poor girls in any shape or form," he confesses. "It sounds twisted as hell, but I can kind of see the logic in what your friend is suggesting. If you can promise me you'll keep those girls safe, then I guess I'm in. My Charlotte would be turning in her grave, God bless her, if I didn't do whatever I could to help those girls."

I think Bert has pretty much summed up the mood in the room, no one wants any part of the trafficking, but right now, it looks like this is the only way to bring it to an end. We're not naive enough to believe that stopping this operation will prevent it happening again, but if we do this right, we can make a dent in their network and make it harder for them.

"What kind of twisted, sick world are we living in?" Cowboy sighs.

"I know," Angel responds. "As soon as we get over one nightmare there's another straight behind it, each time it gets worse."

"I understand how you all feel," Cam joins in. "I'm not sure it will make anyone feel any better, but it's not that long since we shut down a smaller scale set up. Some sleaze bag was kidnapping girls and forcing them into prostitution, but he made a mistake when he flaunted it in front of me. He's no longer a threat and the girls are safe." That seems to raise the spirits around the table a little. Cam goes on to tell us a little about their last operation and I feel reassured that we have these guys here to support us.

We spend the next few hours discussing Bert's normal route and grilling him for as much information as he can remember about each of his encounters with Carnal. Declan manages to talk him through it in such a way that he remembers a lot more than he thought he could. It's pretty slick, and kind of reminds me of the techniques the FBI agents use in Criminal Minds when they're interviewing. It's one of Rebel's favorite shows so I've been subjected to far too many episodes.

It's decided that the Severed team will have to stay in the background and help out in other ways as there's too much risk of them being recognized by Carnal. They're not happy about that, but understand the logic of it, and we've promised them they can be in at the end when we go in to rescue the girls. At that, Declan warns us that we're not going to go into this all guns blazing, it's very much an evidence gathering venture and that when action is needed it will be coming from higher up. We're here to support and monitor and set the groundwork. That causes a few grumbles and moans of discontent. I think the general consensus around the table is that we want to get in there and smash some heads at the end of all this.

"My guy and his team will be heading the overall 'clean up'," Declan advises, "but I'm sure I can persuade him to let you guys handle the local aspect." We all know that the local aspect means Carnal and that appeases us a little, especially the Severed guys who've been through hell at their hands.

"I think we need to put those bastards down once and for all," Cowboy states. "Make sure this time they can't come back."

There's a chorus of "hell yeah' and cheers from around the table.

I sit back as the room starts to clear at the end of the meeting and wonder what the hell we've got ourselves into. I just hope we haven't bitten off more than we can handle.

CHAPTER ELEVEN

Jackson

The past week seems to have flown by and dragged all in equal measure. I spend my nights at the hospital with Sue, and during the day I'm here at the clubhouse helping coordinate the surveillance. I hate the reconnaissance phase; I want to get past it and into the action but understand how necessary it is. I'm absolutely exhausted as I only seem to be grabbing short naps here and there, most of them in that uncomfortable hospital chair at the side of Sue's bed or on one of the sofas in the lounge at the club.

I must have nodded off again as I feel myself being shaken awake by a hand on my shoulder. Looking up groggily it takes me a moment to focus and see that it's Rebel. Shouldn't she be at work? Glancing at my watch shows me it's much later than I thought it was, and I should be heading over to the hospital by now.

"Hey, darlin', sorry, can't stay, I need to get to the hospital," I apologize to her.

"Not so fast old man, you're absolutely shattered. I'm calling time out on you. You need a full night's sleep in your own bed before you collapse on us and end up in a hospital bed next to Sue," Rebel admonishes.

"But…" before I can say anything else Rebel stops me, holding a hand in front of me to prevent me from getting up.

"No, not happening. Sue's still sedated and won't know you're not there, and even if she did know, she'd rather you took care of yourself. I'll sit with her tonight; I don't have any appointments in the morning so can sleep myself when Smokey takes over."

My girl has it all worked out. The old ladies have set up a rota so that Sue is never on her own during the day. The hospital relaxed the rules on next of kin, but she's still only allowed one visitor at a time, and they've told us that it will do her good if she has familiar voices sat talking to her.

As much as I'd love to argue, I know I need to get some proper sleep, I can't risk riding the bike when I'm this tired, it wouldn't just be me I was putting at risk but other road users too. My body feels like a lead weight, it's as though Rebel forcing me to stop has halted the adrenaline that's been keeping me going for the past few days and I suddenly feel so bone weary. I'm not actually sure I'll even make it home in my current state.

Rebel must have read my mind, "I made up your room upstairs with clean sheets for you, you can crash here, you've got stuff in your wardrobe and toiletries in the bathroom." She's right, as Sue and I often stay over here when we've had a club night so we can both enjoy a drink we always keep a few things here just in case.

Rebel walks up with me, somehow she's worked her way in against my body and her head is resting on my shoulder as we walk, my arm holding her into me. I miss this side of her, my little girl has grown up and no longer needs the hugs and cuddles from her dad quite as much as she used to, even if her old man still wants them. It brings back so many happy memories.

Rebel pulls away and opens the door in front of me, she looks a little embarrassed as she points to Sue's things on the dresser. 'I didn't thought about how much of Sue's stuff was still here when I came in to freshen up the bed, but I didn't want to put it away. It felt wrong, do you know what I mean?"

Looking at Sue's things hurts, it's a reminder that she's not here, but more, it's a reminder of how deeply she was entwined in my life before I turned into an idiot and broke it off.

"I can box it up if you'd like?" She offers.

"No, leave it, I've been a bloody idiot and as soon as she wakes up I'm going to put that right, if she'll still have me."

Rebel looks crestfallen for a moment, and instead of the grown woman I know she is, all I can see is a frightened little girl standing in front of me. "She will wake up won't she? She will be all right?"

"Of course she will, darlin'," I pull her into a hug, wrapping my arms around her and holding her close. "That's not just wishful thinking either, Cathy says she's doing well, better than they expected. They just need to keep her asleep a little bit longer while her body heals."

What I don't tell her is they're not sure if we'll get Sue back the way she was. That blow to the head caused them some concern, and they won't know how much damage there was, if any, until they bring her around. I'm trying to stay positive, but deep down I'm scared to hell.

Every night I sit beside her, holding her hand and remind her of all the good times that we've shared, all the things I want to do with her in the future and I apologize repeatedly. I don't know if she can hear me, or if she'll even remember any of it, but if there's the smallest chance that she can then I'll continue to chatter away to her.

I can't imagine a future without Sue in it, and I beat myself up for being the bloody fool that I am, thinking I could get along without her.

Rebel slowly extricates herself from my arms and pushes me in the direction of the ensuite, telling me to go sort myself out and get some sleep.

"I promise I'll take good care of her for you." She reassures me as she slips out of the room.

I look at the shower longingly, I could really do with the hot water on my aching neck and shoulders, but I know what I need right now is sleep. I finish up in the bathroom quickly and head back to the bed. Rebel's changed the sheets so the familiar dimple from Sue's head on her pillow has gone. I hold it to my face anyway, but all I smell is laundry detergent, it no longer smells like Sue. I take a bottle of her perfume from the dresser and spray a little on her pillow before putting it back on the bed. Sad I know, but I can't help it.

It doesn't feel right sleeping in this bed without her, I can't remember the last time I slept here at the clubhouse alone, so I decide to just lay on top of the sheets. I find myself pulling her pillow closer to me, almost hugging it, so I can embrace her smell. I've turned into a fucking pussy and all for a woman. As much as I think the guys in the club would laugh themselves silly if they could see me now, I guess that they'd all understand. The older I've got, the more I've felt that need for a partner, someone to share my life with. It's not easy finding someone who will understand and fit into this lifestyle, I think maybe that could be why Aaron has never settled down, but Sue is a perfect fit for me in all ways. It took almost losing her to grasp that, fool that I am.

Almost as soon as my head hits the pillow my eyes become heavy. There's no point trying to fight it, so I give in, drifting off with memories of Sue laid here beside me.

CHAPTER TWELVE

Jackson

T he club house is a hive of activity when I head down in search of breakfast. I still ache everywhere but I feel much more with it this morning. I feel guilty that I slept so well when Sue is in hospital, but I definitely needed it.

Aaron spots me as I'm heading to the kitchen to see if there's any chance of a cooked breakfast and he joins me. I'm grateful when he tells me I still have time for something to eat before the Church meeting he's arranged. Bert's getting his truck back this morning and is planning on another run to the docks today as per his normal schedule, so we're going to make sure we have all options covered for him.

He could have got it back days ago, but we wanted to give him a few days of respite before Carnal started in on him again. He'd told his neighbor's he was off out of state for a few days to visit an old friend whilst his truck was out of action so if anyone was sniffing around there was a plausible back story. Instead, he's been at Declan's ranch where, alongside keeping him safe, they've been debriefing him as much as possible.

The aroma of bacon, sausage and eggs hits me as soon as I walk into the kitchen, and I smile at Smokey when she hands me a plate full of my favorite things before I've even made it to the table. Aaron complains when he has to fend for himself.

"Be off with you, you lazy bugger, you're big enough and ugly enough to look after yourself," Smokey chastises him. "Our Jackson needs looking after, just look at him, he's practically wasting away with grief." Only Smokey would get away with talking to our Club President like that, although I'm not quite sure where she's got the impression I'm wasting away from.

Aaron walks up and stands right in her face, it would intimidate anyone else but just makes Smokey laugh, at which he pulls her into a warm embrace.

"Good job I love you, you daft old bat," he tells her.

"I need a sick bag, this show of emotion is too much for me," I quip, causing them to break apart, although they're both laughing happily. It's nice to see Smokey smiling again. Losing Bandit hit us all hard, but having been together for so long, I can't imagine how painful that loss must be for her.

"What you need is feeding up," Smokey chastises, walking over and adding an extra rasher of bacon or two to my already overflowing plate.

"Keep feeding him like that and he'll need a bloody heart surgeon instead," jokes Aaron. Smokey harrumphs and turns her back on him, walking away with the rest of the bacon, much to his disgust. She quickly relents when he starts pleading though and his plate soon looks as overfilled as mine.

"Any news?" I ask Aaron from the side of my mouth as it's currently full of bacon. That earns me a reprimand from Smokey for talking with my mouth full. Bloody hell, it's like being a small child again, being supervised whilst I eat. Aaron looks like he's about to reply but as he's still eating he's quickly silenced by a stern look from Smokey.

"Right, I'll leave you two boys to your breakfasts and your war talk. I'm heading to the hospital to sit with Sue," Smokey tells us, walking towards the door to the lounge area, and reminding us to put our dirty dishes in the dishwasher when we're done.

Aaron waits till he's sure she's out of the room and earshot before he replies.

"It's too early, really," he acknowledges. "There've been bits and pieces of intel coming in, but today's the day we're expecting things to get moving. We'll cover it all off in Church, be good to hear your take on things." With that, he returns to demolishing the mountain of breakfast food on his plate, I'm happy to join him in that pursuit.

The room we hold Church in is bursting at the seams again when I enter alongside Aaron, but our seats at the head of the table have been left empty for us. As VP I'm his right-hand man. I nod at Bert as I pass, enough time has passed now that I no longer want to smash his face in for what happened to Sue, but when I see him I always get a flash-back of Sue on the stretcher just before they put her in the helicopter. It's an image I wish I could erase from my memory.

Aaron brings the meeting to order and asks Declan to start it off with his update.

His contact still isn't picking up much chatter about this new network, other than there's a new player on the block. This could mean they're super organized or it could also mean that they're rank amateurs, it's too early to tell just yet. Obviously, we all hope it's the latter, but we need to be prepared. If this is an organized gang then there'll be serious money and muscle behind it.

It seems a massive leap to think that Carnal could have progressed this far from the drug smuggling, gun running and protection rackets, but there's been so much dissent amongst them since they lost their Presi-dent and a lot of infighting for the top spot. Right now, we have to assume that anything is possible and prepare accordingly. Wrath hasn't been able to offer any real insight as his role as enforcer and hitman for hire had kept him away from the internal politics and business decisions. He was never a part of that inner circle at the top.

The tracker's been installed on Bert's truck and hopefully it's hidden well enough that it won't be discovered when Carnal try and modify it to hide their cargo.

Declan confirms that his contact is arranging for some more equipment for us to help with the tracking and monitoring. I'm not quite sure what he does, but he has access to the latest tech, much more advanced than anything we had access to in the Army. It all sounds very secret squirrel to me, but what do I know. It seems more on a scale with Mission Impossible, whereas I reckon most of us never really progressed much beyond Rambo and brute force. There's a chorus of laughter when I say that out loud.

Declan agrees with me, and he's not long left the service himself. He used to serve with him so can vouch for him.

"The guy really came through for us when we took on that drug gang in Severed," Angel tells us. "I don't know what we'd have done if Declan hadn't moved to Severed. I don't think we'd have been able to handle it on our own." There's a lot of respect around the table for the work Declan and his buddies have carried out since they left the Army, although Cowboy is quick to remind us all how much better the local bar is since Declan took it over.

Despite some of the lighthearted comments like Cowboy's about the pub, the mood is still pretty somber. It's been a week, and we don't really seem to have moved forward at all, not to mention we're all on edge at the thought of the girls that are going to get caught up in the trafficking. None of us can bear to think of that side of things. Right now, we all feel pretty helpless. We're out of our depth even with the support of Declan and his high-level contacts.

Trafficking is something you read about and struggle to comprehend can happen in this day and age. Greed is timeless though, and sadly, to some, human life isn't valued as it should be. It's a commodity to be traded as distasteful as the rest of us find it. It's sickening to think that people can be bought and sold and treated worse than cattle in the process.

Bert shows us the route he'll be traveling, and we plot various places where we can have support in place, trying to think where we'd set up an ambush if it was the other way around. Declan cautions that we shouldn't just cover the route Bert's planning, we need to have people ready to adapt if there are any diversions or anything unforeseen. It's a good shout.

It's a good couple of hours before the meeting is called to a close, but I think we've tried to cover everything. Bert looks nervous as hell as he heads off to pick up his truck, I don't blame him. Mind you, that might play in our favor as it will be the kind of behavior the guys from Carnal will be expecting from him.

Let's just hope that when the action starts we can stay back as we've been asked. I know we're all going to struggle with standing by and letting those poor girls suffer. All we can do is hope that this time, the end justifies the means, and too much damage hasn't been done.

Time to get this show on the road.

CHAPTER THIRTEEN

Jackson

F rustrating isn't the word for the last few days. Nothing has happened.

Nothing has changed with Sue and although they're talking about reducing the sedation, they still haven't done it, and nothing has happened on the Bert front either. He's done his runs as normal with no contact from Carnal at all.

There's no way they've given up, but we're at a loss as to why they've backed off. Bert had suggested they'd been shocked by the severity of the accident, but I can't see that. They're not the kind of people to be concerned about anyone getting hurt. I suspect it's more likely them waiting to see if the police interest has waned yet following the investigation into what caused the accident rather than anything else.

Declan's contact has spoken to the local police chief and they've agreed that for now the accident will be put down to a blown tire and recorded as an accident. The news should filter out about that in the next few days, so we just have to sit tight and wait for something to happen.

As you can imagine, waiting is not something that any of us do well.

Tempers are tense, but so far no one has blown up at each other thankfully. I'm not sure how much longer that can last. Everyone's so frustrated at the lack of action.

Rebel has persuaded me to have a couple of nights away from the hospital, and whilst I hate being away, I know she's right. I'll be no use to Sue when she comes round if I'm exhausted, although I'm careful to make sure it's never two nights in a row.

Rebel and Maeve are in the lounge when I get downstairs along with Eve and Teresa from Severed. Maeve is on the floor playing with Teresa's little boy, Aaron. I can't believe how quickly he's growing. They're discussing wedding plans for Eve, and I decide to leave them to it, I'm not interested in all that girly stuff, but Rebel calls me over.

I give my girl a hug and greet everyone else. Aaron crawls over to me and starts tugging at my leg for my attention. I look down at him. "What do you want little man?" He shifts himself to a sitting position and holds his hands up, indicating that he wants me to pick him up. I may be a tough as hell biker and ex-military to boot, but even I can't resist the call of a toddler who wants holding.

I lift him up and straightaway he goes for my beard, there's a surprise, the kid is fascinated by it much to the amusement of the girls. I used to find it funny till the first time he showed me how strong he is and yanked on it. That brought tears to this tough man's eyes I can tell you.

Before I can stop him he's done it again, little bugger. The sting has my eyes watering and Rebel is guffawing with laughter until I remind her she's no better every time she gets her eyebrows done. I went with her once and for the life of me I can't understand why women sit there and have their eyebrows threaded then complain about how much it hurts. Just don't have it done then is my logic!

Before Aaron can go in for a repeat I clasp his little fist in my hand and move it towards my mouth, pretending to eat his fingers. Is there any sweeter sound in the world than the sound of a child's laughter? That gives me an idea. I turn to Teresa.

"Do you think it would be okay to take Aaron in to visit Sue?" I ask her.

Teresa looks a little unsettled by the idea so I'm quick to reassure her. "They've mentioned they're hoping to try bringing her out of the sedation this week, and I was just thinking, once all the machines are gone so it's less scary for him, it might help her want to wake up if she can hear this little guy laugh?"

"I think it's a great idea," Rebel jumps on the idea. "It's just what she needs. I'm sure she's sick of listening to us guys prattling on about nothing."

I can see that Teresa's still not sure but don't want to pressure her. It's her decision at the end of the day, and whilst I'm thinking about what would be best for Sue, she's got to think about what's best for her son.

"Can I think about it?" I admire the girl for not saying no.

"Of course you can, I understand it's not an easy ask, but I do think it might help."

Now I've distracted Aaron from tugging on my beard he's less interested in being in my arms and starts wriggling. I lower him to the floor where his toys are, and he's soon distracted by one of his musical toys. When he starts hammering away at it the noise becomes too much for me, that's one thing I don't miss from Rebel's childhood, so I quickly make my excuses and leave.

There are a few hours before I need to be at the hospital, so I decide to head out to the ranch, I normally check in a few times a week but since Sue's accident I've hardly been by.

The ranch is busting as always when I arrive, a part of me is sad at the number of kids out there who need our help, the ones who come here are only a small fraction of the ones that need us, but I also know how much difference coming here makes. These few kids are getting a chance to see that there is a better world out there.

Smokey collars me almost as soon as I arrive, she's been doing the lunches again today and I can see that something is troubling her.

"What's up?" I ask her as she brews me a cup of coffee. She waits till she's served us both before she sits down at the table with me.

"Just before we lost Bandit, "she pauses a moment, and a look of such loss passes over her face I want to reach out and hug her, but I settle for putting my hand on top of hers to offer her some comfort. "Just before we lost Bandit," she continues, "I suspected something was wrong with one of the girls, Shelby, so I got her to help me in the kitchen and wheedled the problem out of her. Turns out her mom's new boyfriend was getting a little too friendly and she couldn't tell her mom for fear she wouldn't be believed." Smokey takes a sip of her coffee before she continues. "I went with her and supported her while she told her mom, and as I'd expected, her mom was on her side. She kicked that loser to the kerb straight away. Shelby was so much brighter after that; it was like she'd got her shine back. She's been fine for weeks but these last few days she's started looking like she did then, so I took her aside and asked what was wrong. Turns out this creep has been hanging around when mom's not there, standing on the corner watching her when she's walking to the store, under the lamppost across the street from the door. She says all he's doing is watching but it's creeping her out."

"Has she told her mom?," I ask. Smokey shakes her head.

"No, she doesn't want to worry her, she's been trying to ignore him, but I can tell it's really scaring her."

I have another mouthful of coffee before asking, "What do you need from me?"

"I just wondered if one of the guys could keep an eye out on her for me, nothing obvious, just watch out, I'd do it myself but I'm not sure I wouldn't go right up to him and smack him in the mouth."

I almost spit my coffee out at the thought of Smokey smacking the loser, it's exactly the sort of thing she'd do, and it's definitely not going to help the situation.

"I know the timing isn't great, you're all working on that thing with Bert and Severed, but I'm worried about her."

"Leave it with me," I reassure her. She's right we're all busy right now, but I'm sure we can spare someone to ensure the girls safety. We're still waiting on Carnal making a move so should be okay.

Smokey seems more relieved knowing that we're going to look into this, and I finish my coffee with her before heading to the hospital to sit with Sue. Hopefully they'll have some positive news for me on that score, I just want my Sue back.

CHAPTER FOURTEEN

Jackson

L ast night's hospital visit finally gave me some hope. The doctor revealed that Sue has been doing better than they'd expected and they're looking to reduce her sedation by the end of the week if she continues improving.

I admit it's been so hard sitting there, talking away to her, but getting absolutely no response and no sign she can even hear me. I have to believe Cathy when she tells me I'm not wasting my time.

I've only just woken up and I rub my eyes, trying to clear the sleep from them. I promised Smokey yesterday that we'd look into the creep that's been bothering Shelby, and I need to get one of the guys onto it. If Smokey thinks something is off, then I'm going to listen to her. It's rare she ever asks anything of us, her and Bandit have always been independent. I have to stop and remind myself that I can't think of Bandit in the present tense. His loss still hurts deeply. Bandit hiding his cancer from the rest of us was just another example of how stubborn he was. I wish he'd come to us, told us. Not that there is anything we could have done to prevent his passing, but at least we could have been there for him a bit more over his last few weeks.

That's typical Bandit, trying to protect the rest of us. I wonder if having extra time to prepare ourselves for his passing would have made any difference rather than the sudden shock of losing him the way we did. Either way wouldn't have spared us the pain of losing him, though. Perhaps knowing in advance would have given us a chance to spend more time with him, to have said goodbye at least. I know Bandit would have hated us fussing over him, so perhaps I get why he decided not to tell us after all.

Smokey is still a shadow of her former self. It's good that she's finally back at the ranch now, but the spark has gone from her eyes. She may think she's fooling everyone, but I can see through the facade she's putting on. I wish I could help her, but I'm at a loss where to start. I can't imagine what it must be like losing your other half after so many years together. I know how painful it's been for me seeing Sue in that hospital bed, and we've hardly been together any time in the grand scheme of things, and let's be honest, thanks to my stupidity we're not really together right now, although that's something I plan on putting right as soon as she wakes up. I'm determined I'm going to fix this and get her back.

The mood in the clubhouse is off. It has been since Sue's accident, especially coming so soon after losing Bandit. The guys are frustrated that we're in a holding pattern right now, waiting for something to happen. This inactivity is driving them all crazy. I need to get my head back in the game. I've been too distracted by Sue to fully concentrate on what's happening around here, or not happening, as is the case currently. It's a good job nothing's been happening as my focus isn't on what's going on around here and it should be.

Some guys from Severed are in the clubhouse when I go down in search of coffee and Cowboy indicates he wants a word. I wonder if he has some news on the creep who's been hassling Shelby. They'd offered to take a few shifts watching him for us to help us out.

I grab a coffee for me and a fresh one for Cowboy and take a seat opposite him. We both take a moment to enjoy the coffee before saying anything other than basic greetings.

"It's always good coffee when I come here," Cowboy looks satisfied, but his face quickly becomes serious. "I think we need a couple more days on this guy you've had us following, but I think there's something there."

I'm mid sip when I hear him and quickly put my cup down in surprise. If I'm honest, I thought it would be nothing.

"What makes you think that?" I ask.

"First, it's the way he's been acting. He's definitely watching the lass and trying to do it covertly but he's bloody useless. No wonder she thought he was following her," he pauses a moment. "We think he's involved with Carnal somehow as well. We haven't had eyes on a meeting with them yet, but he's definitely been in the same bars as them and that sounds too much like a coincidence to me."

"What the hell would he be mixed up with Carnal for? It's not like they're local to the area." I ponder.

"Exactly, but sure as hell, if he's into anything with them, then it's going to be nasty." Cowboy looks serious but having heard what went down with Carnal in the past, I can't say I'm surprised.

I guess we've been lucky that they've never been on our radar, but the news that they're active in our local area is concerning. That, coupled with all the infighting we've heard about, doesn't bode well.

"I think we need to raise this at the next meeting, just as a precaution," I suggest. "My gut tells me we need to pay closer attention to this guy." With everything else going on, this had been a pretty low-key observation just to keep Smokey happy.

"I agree. There's something there, and we need to figure it out. He was a slime bag before we knew what creeps he's hanging around with." Cowboy concedes.

I'm glad we have people like Smokey helping at the ranch, able to perceive that things aren't as they should be with some of the kids and prepared to follow through on it. We all detest abusers and will do what we can to keep our own safe. I know there won't be a shortage of volunteers when we ask for bodies to follow and observe this guy.

Aside from my years in the military, I've been lucky. Life's been pretty good to us all here at Hellion mostly, but there's been a change these past few years that we've all felt. The world is getting that bit harsher, and trouble has started lurking on our doorstep. Like Severed, we've always been a peaceful club, nothing like the 1%'ers that you hear about, and the media sensationalizes. That bloody series *Sons of Anarchy* made those villains headliners, women swooned over them, and I never have and never will understand that appetite for violence.

Thinking of the show reminds me of a conversation I'd had with Rebel about it. Considering she's what I assume would be the target audience, she did nothing but complain about the number of times they showed the main characters naked ass. "It's not even bloody attractive," she'd complained, her voice laced with disgust, "and as for his bloody whiny wife! The best character is the mother by far." She'd then warned me she'd bought a carving fork and given me a knowing look. Having not understood what she was on about, I'd eventually given in and watched the scene where the mother used it as a weapon. Wow, I'll never be able to look at a carving fork again without that image popping up.

Cowboy and I catch up on what's been happening, and no, it's not gossip, despite what Rebel constantly tells me. I always throw back that we're grown men and grown men don't gossip, they simply have an exchange of information. That's my story and I'm sticking to it.

CHAPTER FIFTEEN

Rebel

With everything that's been happening lately, we decided a girl's night was needed. It feels like forever since we got together with Eves stripper friends from England, and yet it's only been a few months. That said, it's long enough that Eve's pregnancy is starting to show. She has a tiny baby bump and she and Angel are so excited to meet their new arrival. She's had the first scan but doesn't want to know whether it's going to be a boy or a girl. They want a surprise. The rest of us want to know so we can plan our shopping and have a baby shower properly. They won't even do a gender reveal party, spoilsports.

It feels weird having a girl's night without Sue, but hopefully she'll be able to join us for the next one. I know she's not out of the woods yet, but I've decided that she's going to get better, although I know wishes alone won't make that happen.

The night has been tamer than previous ones, because of the mocktails Eve and Teresa are drinking, and partly because of a joint concern for Sue and the events that led to her accident.

Eve had been telling us about the difference between her mom and Teresa's mom growing up. I know for a long time Eve didn't get on with her mom and it's only since she met Angel that her mom has stepped up and become a decent woman.

"It must have been weird for you growing up without a mom, Rebel," Eve half comments, half asks.

"I never felt I missed out," I confess, "if anything I felt other kids missed out by only having one dad, although no matter how many dads I have, if Jackson declared no, that was that. I could try to con one of the others into agreeing but somehow they always knew." I laugh.

"Is it strange having your mom back in your life?" Eve asks. "I know how strange it's been for me getting used to the change in my mom. She's not being a bitch all the time anymore."

"When she first showed up, I was so angry with her, I wanted nothing to do with her." It seems strange now looking back on what was such an unsettling time in my life. "All my life I'd built her up to be this evil woman, she'd abandoned me, and it took a while for me to under-stand that she'd done that to protect me, and she had wanted me, but she'd never have been able to keep me." I can see nods of understanding around the table.

"I'm not sure if we really have a mom/daughter relationship yet, or if we'll ever get there with time. It's weird to explain but I think it's easier to think of her as a really good older friend rather than a mom, I've not had long to grasp the fact I have a mother, whereas she's had all my life knowing she had me and loved me."

"I get that," Eve agrees. "I really wanted my mom to love me growing up, and I struggled to love her back because time after time she let me down and failed me, I always wanted Teresa's mom and dad to adopt me, they were my idea of a perfect family."

"Am I the only one that grew up with both parents then?" Teresa looks surprised when she looks around the table and recognize that she's the odd one out.

"Yep, my mom died in an accident when I was really little," Maeve confides. "I don't really remember her, and I've never known my dad, so I ended up in the system till I was turned out at eighteen. That's why I like to help out at the ranch, I feel a real affinity for those kids, and I hope that my helping them will mean they have a better shot at life than me."

From being a night to celebrate being with each other the mood at the table has definitely dropped, there's not one of us sat here who has had an easy or a normal life. Even Teresa who grew up with both parents lost her mom to cancer before she left home. It's quite sobering.

"Do you know anything about your dad?" I turn to Maeve.

"Nope, mom had put unknown on my birth certificate and there was nothing in her papers to say who he was or that she'd had any communication with anyone who might have been my dad." Maeve distracts herself by twirling the straw round in her drink.

"Have you ever tried to find out?" I'm curious, but I also have the inkling of an idea brewing.

"I wouldn't know where to start, would you?" She seems to ask the whole table.

"I might have an idea," I start, but pause. I haven't asked her if she would want to know. "Is it something you'd like to know? I think I'd have been happy never knowing who my mom was before I met her." It's such a personal thing, not all kids want to know who their unknown parents are. For others, I know it's a lifelong yearning, that wanting to know where they come from.

"I'm not sure," Maeve hesitates, "it's never been something I thought was possible, so I guess I haven't given it much thought. What if I find out and he's an ass or he could be a really great guy but not want to know me?"

"Good points, I hadn't thought of it like that. What do you guys think?" I pose the question to the rest of the table.

"I get the wanting to know but afraid of the answer," Eve contributes. "I never knew my dad and all I have is my mom's assertion that he was an asshole. She says he walked out on us, so I guess he wasn't the kind of guy I'd want to find, but then I guess my mom could have told me a pack of lies."

I can see that it's something she's not thought about seriously either. I'm not really sure how we ended up on this topic, but I've now got an idea that will help not only me, but Maeve as well. Perhaps if I suggest it as a group idea I can get the answers I want without arousing suspicion from the others.

"Well, I was just thinking, why don't we all buy one of those DNA tests. You know the ones that tell you who you're related to and what your make up is? I'm pretty sure my ancestry will trace back to the English convict ships, but I think it might be fun, not to mention, maybe Eve and Maeve could find out who their dads are?" I pose it as a question.

"How do they work?" Maeve asks, "I'm not a fan of needles, I don't need to do a blood test, do I? And how would they find someone I don't know?"

"One of my clients did one, and they were telling me they found relatives they didn't know they had all over the world. If the other person has taken a test and they share any DNA with you, it will come back as a match. I'm pretty sure it's just a cheek swab." I explain.

"How much are they? They sound expensive?" I can tell that Maeve is interested, but I also know she doesn't have a lot of money after her ex wiped her out.

"I'll get them, my treat, seeing as it was my idea," I offer. "We could get them for our other halves as well. What do you think?" I think this solves half my Christmas present list as well as giving me answers, so it's a win-win for me.

"I'm in." Teresa raises her mocktail in a toast. "I can't wait to see if I'm related to the Queen of England."

"Count me in too," Eve raises her glass, 'although I reckon I'm more likely to be related to the Queen's scullery maid." We all laugh at that.

"Go on then," Maeve lifts her glass as well.

"Leave it with me. Here's to us and finding answers to our past." I clink my glass to each of the others in a toast.

The mood lifts for the rest of the evening, especially for me, knowing that I might have the answers I need without hurting anyone's feelings in the process.

CHAPTER SIXTEEN

Jackson

I'm sitting in the backyard at Rebel's enjoying a cold beer with Chris, her partner. It feels like forever since I've seen him, as he's been away on business quite a lot recently. I'm glad he's here, as I'd thought these frequent business trips were an excuse to escape a failing relationship, but I'm pleased to find out I was wrong. Hardly surprising, I got it wrong about Sue as well. I'm not exactly the best judge of relationships, am I?

Chris is asking for my advice. He's been having to spend so much time away as he's still tying up his late father's estate. Unfortunately, his late father was an asshole who tried to bully and blackmail my girl for some land that I'd given her. He almost destroyed Dee Dee as well.

Luckily for us all, he's dead, and yet his legacy is still causing Chris issues. Chris and Dee Dee have been trying to trace as many of the people that the creep had blackmailed as they can and make some form of restitution. His father didn't acknowledge Chris until his last few years when he needed him to carry out his dirty work, threatening Chris when he was at his most vulnerable. Chris's mom was seriously ill and needed specialist medical care. The slime ball agreed to pay for it, but on condition Chris worked for him, then constantly threatened him with removing his mom from her nursing home to make him carry out some heinous tasks. Chris had grown up in poverty, just him and his mom, despite the immense wealth his father enjoyed. Money isn't something that ever-interested Chris, nor the politics that were tied up with it all. He's always been happy to pay his own way in life, and he only ever wanted enough to ensure that his mom was looked after when she fell ill. He's concerned that if he stops this search so he can spend more time with Rebel that she'll be disappointed in him, as he's already turned his back on the money. "Did you have money when you first met her?" I remind him. "You didn't have a pot to piss in, yet she looked past that, didn't she?" She looked past a heck of a lot more, including him drugging her the first night they met. "Did she turn her back on Dee Dee when she decided she didn't want any of that blood money?"

"Yeah, I guess." Chris definitely isn't himself.

"And what was the first thing Rebel did when I gave her that land? Did she sell it?" I remind him.

"No, she set up the ranch for the kids."

"Exactly. Rebel isn't greedy. Like you, she's happy with her lot and she wanted to do something good, give back to kids who didn't have the advantages she had growing up." The condensation on the can I'm holding is getting a bit much, so I place it down on the table beside me.

"I guess I'm scared. For me, she's the one, that special girl you only get one chance with and, like you say, I almost blew it straight out of the blocks. I want to give her the moon if she'd let me." He runs his hands through his hair, mussing it up. "I know deep down she understands why I'm away so much, but what's the point of it all if it means I never get to see the woman I love?"

"I think that money can be the best of things sometimes, but at others, it really is the root of all evil. Money can buy you things, but money alone can't buy you memories. People don't remember things, not really. They remember the people and the emotions. That's what really makes a memory. The most valuable gift you can give someone you love is your time." Wow, look at me, I almost sound as though I know what I'm talking about.

"There's still so much money to give back," I can tell he's given this a lot of thought. "And trying to trace where it needs to be returned and manage it all is a full-time job. I'd much rather work at the ranch full time and be here with Rebel."

"Just how much are we talking?" I ask. I'm sure Chris is making this a lot more complicated than it should be. When he passes a piece of paper over, I have to do a double take. That many zeros can't be right. No wonder he's stressed. "Wow!" The word seems very insignificant compared to the effect it's had on me.

"Exactly. I don't think any of us comprehended just how much there would be. It was all squirreled away in tax havens and the like. We know that a lot of it came from blackmail and bribes, but it's so time intensive tracking all this down." It's not a legacy he can be proud of. I know only a handful of people know who his father was, and Chris wants to keep it that way, but still make good on the wrongs his father committed.

"Get a private investigator," I suggest.

"I thought about that, but then we need one we can really trust, as this is such a sensitive issue." He looks perplexed.

"Well, why don't you have a word with Declan? The guys from Severed have a lot of time for him and I think he'd know who you could talk to and trust. He seems to have the right connections." I sound like I know what I'm talking about, but I'm nowhere near qualified to offer advice on this.

"Yeah, I guess. I just haven't been able to think straight since he died. My entire world turned upside down in a few hours and it hasn't righted itself yet." He suddenly looks nervous. "That leads me on to the next thing. I've got something I need to ask you." He's wringing his hands.

"Fire away." I offer. I've no idea what other advice I can offer him.

"I want to ask your permission to ask Rebel to marry me, your blessing." He rushes the words out. Did I just hear him right?

"Let me get this straight. You've just told me you haven't been able to think straight since that dickhead died and now you want to ask Rebel to marry you?" I'm not sure whether to laugh or shake some sense into him. "Do you think she'd say yes?" I genuinely don't know what she'd say. I guess I've just never seen her as the marrying kind. She's always been so stubbornly independent.

"I get it, but Rebel is the one thing I know is right in my life. I don't want to spend another day without her. When I'm away, I miss her like crazy. I catch myself turning to show her something or tell her something, and she's not there. It feels like I'm missing a part of myself."

"She's not pregnant, is she?" She hasn't been herself since Sue's accident, and it's a sudden thought that makes sense of this crazy conversation I'm having with Chris.

"No, nothing like that. I just don't want to waste any more time without her knowing how much she really means to me." Chris reassures me.

I envy Chris. I've never felt that sure about a woman in my life. I've come close twice, once when Rebel was young and I stupidly let it go, and now with Sue, and even then I almost lost it.

"Honestly, it's not my decision to make, my permission to give. I love that girl so much, but I don't know how she'll respond to you. I'm not even sure she's the marrying kind.

You know how fiercely stubborn and independent she is." Chris looks absolutely crestfallen, so I try to dial it in a bit. "That said, I like you. I think you're good for my girl, and if it's what she wants, then I am more than happy to give you my blessing and welcome you into this crazy family. You know what you're getting yourself into if she says yes, don't you?"

Chris laughs for the first time since I got here, a look of relief on his face. "I think what you guys have is beyond amazing and I'd be honored to be a part of that family. I hear what you're saying. I get it. If I ask and she says no, then at least she'll know how important she is to me, how much she means and as long as she'll want me in her life, then I'll settle for that. That said, I'm going to hope that she's not as stubborn as you think, and she'll consider saying yes."

"Fair enough. Have you thought about when you're going to ask her?"

"I haven't got that far ahead," he acknowledges, "I need to pick my moment, but I'm not going to wait too long."

There's the sound of a car pulling up outside and Chris looks over at me, concern on his face.

"That's Rebel, please say nothing about the proposal," he pleads. "No problem." I agree.

Rebel soon joins us in the yard, bringing more cold beers with her. She knows us so well.

CHAPTER SEVENTEEN

Rebel

There's a guilty silence when I ask them what they've been talking about, but then I spot the paperwork on the table and work out it's been about the money trail. My heart breaks for Chris. Not only was his dad an asshat, but he's the one who's left trying to make things right. I wish he could just walk away from it, be free of that bloody man, but I know his conscience won't let him and have to tell him.

"I wish you could walk away from this, babe. I hate that he's still dragging you down." I gesture to the papers as I ignore the empty chair and sit on Chris's lap instead.

"I think Jackson might have had a good idea," Chris looks hopeful rather than resigned. It makes a nice change, as I can't remember the last time I saw that look on his face.

"Oh, yeah?" I look at Jackson hoping that it's a bloody good idea.

"He suggested I have a word with Declan. He should know someone we can trust to be discreet with this." As he's talking, he's unconsciously rubbing his hand along my thigh. I wish he wouldn't as it's really making me wish Jackson wasn't here, so I could take this further.

"That's not a bad idea at all," I reply, putting my hand on top of his to halt the movement. It's been a while, too long, since we had the chance to be intimate. I'm desperate to rip his clothes off and hate that now is most definitely not the time. "I know the guys over at Severed rate him really highly. Things might have been a lot worse for them if he hadn't stepped in to help them. Sue has a lot of time for him as well."

Jackson looks slightly put out when I mention Sue respecting Declan. I wish he'd wake up and comprehend what she means to him and do something about it. I'll give him a little longer to see sense, and if he still does nothing, then I'll step in. As much as I love him, he can be a bloody fool sometimes.

"That's settled then," Chris sounds so relieved and I'm sure his shoulders release just a little of the tension that's been plaguing him.

"Any news on what's happening with Carnal?" I turn to Jackson.

"Not really. They're keeping a pretty low profile at the moment. We still can't figure out who they're working for just yet, but we think we may have found one of their scouts." Both Chris and I sit up and pay attention. "It's nothing definite yet, but Shelby mentioned to Smokey she thought she was being followed. It's that douche that was hanging around with her mother." At my look of concern, he's quick to reassure me. "We've got eyes on him, but we've seen him hanging out in the same bars as Carnal, not that we've seen him in conversation with them yet."

"That's not good," now I'm concerned. "Is Shelby safe?" I care about every single kid that goes to the ranch. I've never thought of myself as maternal before, but when I'm with those kids, I see a side of me I never thought I would.

"Yeah, we've got someone watching all the time now. Severed are helping as well, seeing as they're more familiar with who the Carnal guys are." Jackson reassures me.

"I don't know why I thought they'd be bringing in the girls from outside the area?" I'm confused now. "Surely they wouldn't be stupid enough to foul on their own doorstep?"

"This isn't their home turf, though." Jackson reminds me. "They're based on the other side of Severed to us, and I guess they've had enough run-ins with Severed to want to avoid them."

"I guess." I'm not convinced. I'm worried about the kids at the ranch, Shelby in particular.

"Declan's joining us for a meeting tomorrow at the Club-house. We can see what he thinks the risk might be and if he has any suggestions about security at the ranch that we haven't considered." Jackson suggests.

"I think that's a good idea. We want the kids to feel safe, but we also need to make sure that they don't feel they're constantly being watched." Chris offers.

"Yeah, perfect." I agree. I'm pretty sure the ranch is safe, but it won't do any harm to get a second opinion. As Chris suggested, there's a fine balance to consider.

"So, what's the story with Shelby? Why is he following her? Smokey hasn't mentioned anything to me about it?" I'm not as hands on at the ranch as I'd like to be. It's hard for me not to get involved in the day to day, but I trust Dee Dee to handle it.

Jackson tells us how Smokey had persuaded Shelby to tell her what was wrong and how she'd followed it through and supported her.

"I'm so glad that poor girl has her mom on her side. There are far too many cases where the mom sides with the abuser." I 'm so bloody angry. It's so hard for these kids to open up to an adult and let them know what they're suffering, but then to be told they're a liar just doesn't bear thinking about. As much good as the ranch does, there are so many kids that don't get the help they need or the chances that they deserve. Their lives mapped out by an accident of birth, leaving them without access to the necessities they need, such as love, food, warmth and shelter, often even education.

The ranch hasn't been open that long really, but we're already seeing the positive effect it's having on the kids we support. Better grades, better health, and the best one for me, seeing them smile when before they came to us it was as though they'd forgotten how. We've given them a safe environment and we're teaching them the skills to survive and also improve their lot in life.

"I think I might talk to Declan about some classes for the kids, basic self-defense and the things they need to be aware of in their environment. What do you think?" I have the bit between my teeth now.

"I'm pretty sure the guys have covered some of this stuff already, but it won't do any harm to go over it again. A lot of the kids we work with already have street smarts, but not all of them, and it would be good to get them to be more aware of what's happening to the people around them as well." Jackson agrees with me.

"I just wish we didn't have to have places like the ranch, that kids weren't in a position where they need us. It feels like some of these parents treat their kids as something disposable or just ignore them altogether." I'm so worked up now.

"I know, darlin', but that's the way the world is going. Lucky for those kids, you have got the ranch, and you also have people around you that will support you with it and look out for them, too." As he finishes speaking Jackson's stomach rumbles loudly making us all laugh.

"Anyway," he looks over to the barbecue. "I thought you invited me over here to feed me, not chew my ear off all night." He smirks.

Chris tries to push me off his lap so he can get up and I mutter, but not for long. I soon move to an empty chair. My stomach isn't far off complaining as I was so busy today I worked through lunch again.

"Sure, you don't want me to man the grill?" Jackson offers. I know he's jesting. He does it every time he comes over, as Chris is so territorial about his barbecue. It's man's work, he keeps telling me. I leave him to it, happy to let someone else take the strain for a change. Besides, I'll show him what man's work is later, when Jackson's gone, and I have him all to myself. He's in for a very busy night if I have anything to do with it.

CHAPTER EIGHTEEN

Jackson

The hospital has called as Sue is coming round. The journey feels like it's happening in slow motion and is taking an eternity, even though I know it's probably just the same as normal.

It's early evening and I'm grateful the car park is quieter than during the day when all the outpatient appointments mean it's often packed to capacity. I park up the bike in a spot fairly close to the door, for which I'm grateful. When I get there, the lift is on the ground floor, ready and waiting for me. It's as though things are finally looking up and I choose to take it as a good omen that things will be alright between me and Sue.

Sue's in a side room off the main ward. I'm shown there by the nurse who rang me. As we walk, she tries to prepare me for what's ahead. I hardly listen to her, too excited to see Sue, and too stupid to take in what I should be hearing.

She's trying to warn me that Sue won't be herself for a while yet, but I don't want to believe that.

I should have listened. When I enter the room, the machines have all gone and Sue lies pale against the white sheets, too pale. I think I'd assumed she'd have a bit more color now she was coming round. The nurse is telling me that Sue has been in and out of consciousness for most of the afternoon, only coming round for a couple of minutes at a time. She's pretty disoriented and so far hasn't really grasped what's happened to her. They're not sure if she even understands where she is yet.

Realizing that nearly everything she's told me is negative, the nurse tries to end on a positive, letting me know that it's still early days and they hope Sue will make a full recovery eventually.

Eventually is too long a timeline for me. It's already been too long. I want the old Sue back with me now. I never stated I was a patient man. I want to scoop her into my arms, hug her tight and tell her everything is going to be okay. I don't, as she still looks too fragile for me to try. Instead, I pull the chair a little closer to the bed and settle in beside her, taking her hand in mine and just sit there, watching and waiting.

Everything may have gone my way downstairs, but now we're back in slow motion. I sit there for a couple of hours; the nurses checking in every so often, but Sue stays asleep. I've almost nodded off when I feel her hand move against mine. I sit up, alert, and tighten my grip so she can feel I'm there.

"Sue, darlin', I'm here. You're going to be okay. Come back to me darlin', it's killing me not hearing your voice." Her eyelids flutter and open, her head turning slightly towards me. It's obvious from the panicked expression on her face she doesn't recognize me and pain lances through my heart.

She's trying to speak, but her throat is still raw from the breathing tube that had been keeping her breathing since the accident. She can't get the words to come out and that distresses her even more.

I keep pressing the call button for the nurse, wishing they would hurry and get here. I don't think anyone has ever looked at me with such fear in their eyes. This can't be right. They told me Sue was going to be okay. Why can't she recognize me?

Finally, the nurse that escorted me to the room comes in. She stands on the other side of the bed to where I'm sitting and replaces my hand with her own. Patting Sue's hand gently, she persuades her to look at her instead.

"Hey, lovely. How are you feeling?" Sue tries to speak, but it's just a dry croak, nothing legible. "Your lips must be so dry. Let me get you some water." Rather than give Sue the glass to drink from as she's still laid down, she wets a sponge and gently applies it to Sue's lips. "Is that better?" Sue nods her head slightly, and the nurse repeats the motion a few times, allowing water to drip between her lips. "Do you know where you are?" The nurse questions, her voice low and calming all the time. Sue shakes her head to show that she doesn't, but it's such a small movement, its barely discernible and even that looks to cause her discomfort.

The nurse keeps hold of Sue's hand and sits just on the edge of the bed, not too close to cause her any pain, but close enough she's offering comfort. God, how I envy that nurse right now. "You had a nasty accident, but you're in the hospital now and you're going to be fine." She reassures Sue. "Can you tell me your name, lovely?"

"S...S...Sue," my woman eventually croaks out, barely any volume to her words.

"That's great, Sue." The nurse praises her. "You were pretty banged up when you came into us, so we had to put you to sleep for a while, to give you a chance to heal. That meant you had a breathing tube, and that's why your throat will be so sore right now. It will wear off, and when you're feeling a little stronger, we'll sit you up a bit and give you a drink of water. Are you in pain right now? Do you need any medication?"

Sue raises her other hand to her head. You can tell she's barely any strength as it soon flops back onto the sheet. "Is your head hurting?" The nurse queries as she picks up the chart from the side of the bed, assessing what medication Sue's allowed. "The doctors already prescribed you some painkillers, so give me a moment and I'll go get them for you. You just close your eyes and rest a moment. I'll be right back."

I'm about to ask the nurse a question when she silences me with a look. Sue's eyes have closed and I daren't disturb her. The nurse doesn't take long to come back with a syringe. I've no idea what's in it, but I assume it's pain relief. Once she's administered it, she pats Sue's hand and tries to persuade her to open her eyes again.

"Sue, can you open your eyes for me, lovely?"

Sue's eyes flutter open again. She looks towards me first and still looks petrified, quickly turning back to face the nurse, the sudden movement obviously causing her discomfort from the distressed moan she makes.

"Can you remember where you are, lovely?" The nurse asks. I've no idea why she's asking the same question she did just a few minutes ago and wait with bated breath for the answer.

"H..hospital." Sue eventually replies.

"That's right, lovely. That's great that you remember. Would you like a little more water?" At Sue's nod, she picks up the sponge and repeats the process from earlier. Turning to me, she explains they don't want to give her too much water too quickly, as her body probably wouldn't accept it. Sue shakes her head when she's had enough, and the nurse replaces the sponge in the glass beside the bed.

"You're doing really well, lovely. Now why don't you say hello to this handsome man who's barely left your bedside since they brought in you." The nurse points to me and Sue turns her head to look at me, but it's a look of fear on her face still.

"I… I.. I don't know who he is." She finally croaks out.

CHAPTER NINETEEN

Jackson

I've no idea how long I've been pacing the corridor having been asked to leave Sue's room, it feels like an eternity, but I know it can't have been.

While I'm pacing, a doctor goes into the room, brushing past me in the corridor without acknowledging me. I'm sure I've seen him on several visits and the lack of recognition only serves to further distance me from Sue. I pull my phone out and try calling Rebel, when she doesn't answer I send her a text to let her know that Sue has come round. I don't tell her yet that Sue can't remember me as I know she'll start stressing and worrying about me and I don't want that.

Finally, the doctor leaves the room, ignoring me again and rushing off to what I guess is his next patient. The nurse doesn't come out and I tentatively stick my head around the door. Sue looks to be asleep thankfully, and the nurse, noticing me, turns and gestures for me to stay outside.

"I'll be with you in a minute," she offers, her voice laced with sympathy. That doesn't bode well.

Returning to the corridor I lean against the wall and wonder what all of this means for my future. I'd been so focused on fixing things with Sue and her getting better that I hadn't really thought about what would happen if she woke up and didn't want me. I never for one minute thought she wouldn't recognize me.

Eventually the nurse comes out and suggests we head for the visitors room on this floor. I guess the fact she isn't telling me to leave is a positive sign, at least I hope it is.

I follow her down the corridor and into the sparse room. It's such an impersonal space, plain white walls and slightly shabby furniture although they have tried to make it comfortable. The nurse notices me staring at the worn arms on the sofa, I'm not really taking them in, they're just something to focus on as there are no pictures on the wall other than some tattered posters about washing. your hands.

"I know it's not much," she apologizes, "rooms like this are funded from donations and there are a lot of rooms and not a lot of money. It tends to be the cancer ward that gets the donations.

"Oh, no, I," I stall for a moment, "I wasn't thinking that" I'm quick to reassure her. "To be honest, I'm not sure I'm really thinking at all right now, this has come as a bit of a shock." She gestures for me to take a seat and sits in the armchair across from the coffee table that faces the sofa.

"I totally understand," she reassures me. "The thing is, when the brain gets injured we can't always predict the outcome, and sometimes it shuts down to protect itself. Just because Sue can't remember you now doesn't mean that this is going to be a permanent situation." She sees the look of relief on my face but quickly dashes it with her next words. "That said, we can't promise that part of her memory will ever come back. Right now, it's a waiting game. The good news is that Sue does seem to be alert, her speech is still there, she seems able to understand what we're saying to her, and she knows who she is. These are all positive signs."

"She doesn't know me, that's not positive for me," I retort. Realizing how angry my words sounded I'm quick to apologize. "I'm sorry, that wasn't called for. I do appreciate everything you guys are doing for her and that you've got her through this so far."

"It's okay, honestly, I understand, and I've seen people react much more strongly than you when this has happened before. It's got to be hard for you. I get that. I'm afraid I can't give you a timeline right now or even promise you that she will get that memory back. What I can tell you is that she's asking for Teresa and Elvis. Are those names familiar to you?" She looks over at me to see if I recognize them.

I groan out loud, she doesn't even know Elvis is dead. "Elvis is her old partner and Teresa is his daughter, she knew them when she lived in Severed before she came to Maldon and met me." I offer.

"That's great," she starts. "Are you able to get hold of them, if she sees them that might help start rebuilding some of her memory." She suggests.

"Elvis was killed a couple of years ago now, will finding that out make it worse?" I ask. "I can get Teresa to come visit her, and a few of the other people that she knew and was close to when she was there," I offer.

"Certainly, get the others to come visit if you can," she stops to think for a moment. "I'll have to check with the doctor about what and when to tell her about Elvis, but I can find that out for you before they visit."

"So, what happens about me?" I ask, I know that sounds selfish but that's how I feel right now. This whole thing is so unfair, why isn't it me she's asking for. "We'd had a falling out just before the accident, do you think that may be why she can't remember me?" I'm grasping at anything here that can give me hope.

"I honestly can't say, it's common in traumatic accidents like Sue had for there to be some short-term memory loss. I don't want to give you false hope though. I can't promise you that she'll get that level of memory back. It's a waiting game."

I laugh, bitterly. "This has been one long waiting game already, ever since the accident."

"I know," she empathizes. "No two recoveries are the same though, the same way no two injuries are ever quite the same. All I can remind you of is that there are plenty of positive signs here, this could have been so much worse."

A shudder goes through me at the thought of how much worse this could have been, various scenarios flash through my mind, some in graphic detail. I need to hold on to the thought that Sue has survived a horrific accident, the broken bones will heal, and it looks like she's going to be okay. We have to focus on the positives here, the nurse is right. I can't lose myself in selfish pity right now, I still need to be there for Sue, even if it isn't face to face. "Okay, what can I do to help?"

"As I explained, if you can get hold of the friends she can remember and ask them to come visit that's a great first step, however," she pauses a moment, "I think its best if you don't visit her for a while yourself."

I nod my head slowly, understanding even if I'm struggling to accept it.

"What about any of her new friends, are they allowed to visit?" I just hope that seeing Rebel may help her remember but that hope is quickly dashed as well.

"I think, until Sue remembers something from this new period in her life we'll have to stick to just visitors from the time that she remembers, I'm sorry." I can see from her face how genuine her sympathy is, but right now that doesn't help me much. How the hell am I going to tell the others about this?

CHAPTER TWENTY

Eve

"Eve, there's a call for you!" Angel shouts across the clubhouse, waving his mobile at me. Who can be calling me on his phone? He pulls me in and kisses me before passing the phone whispering that it's Jackson on the other end.

"Hello?" I ask hesitantly.

"Hi Eve, thanks for taking my call. I've got some good news and some bad news for you." Angel must see the look of alarm on my face but pats my arm, reassuring me. Has he already heard the news? "Sue's woken up."

"That's fantastic news," I interrupt him then remember he mentioned there was bad news as well. "What's the bad news?" A chill runs through my body, fear at what he's going to say to me next.

"She doesn't remember me; she doesn't seem to have any memories from her time here in Maldon." I can hear the sorrow in his voice and my heart goes out to him.

"Is she okay otherwise?" I rush out.

"Yeah, the doctors seem pretty pleased with the progress she's making, the issue is that she's asking for Elvis and Teresa, she doesn't know Elvis is dead." I almost drop the phone in shock but quickly gather myself together.

"What can I do to help?" I offer.

"Well, I'm hoping that as Teresa's best friend you could let her know, you might be able to find a way of telling her that doesn't cause too much hurt when you tell her about Sue thinking Elvis is still alive."

I have no idea where the hell to start with that conversation but rush to agree. "Of course I will, I'll figure something out. I'll talk to Prez, he may be able to help. Anything else we can do?"

"The hospital has asked everyone here to stay away for now and that she only has visitors from the time that she remembers, could you sort that out at your end?" I can't begin to imagine how hard this must be on her new family, not even allowed to visit, when it was so clear in that waiting room the night of the accident just how much Sue means to them all already.

"Of course I will, I'm sure we'll have plenty of people eager to visit her now she's awake. I'll be one of the first on that list." I'm eager to see Sue, but suddenly wonder if she'll know me, after all I arrived just before Elvis died.

"Thanks, Eve. I really appreciate it. Angel has my number, if you can let me know how the visits go. It's killing me not being able to go and see her."

"Of course I will," I promise. Jackson tells me goodbye and the call ends. Angel looks at me expectantly. "How much do you know?"

Angel pulls me over to a quiet corner of the clubhouse and we sit down, as usual Angel doesn't let me sit beside him but sits me on his lap. As soon as we're sat down his hand covers my baby bump protectively. He's a bloody cave-man, but he's my caveman and I'm so grateful for the day that I met him, even if it almost killed me.

"Jackson told me what happened before I called you over, he rang me as he didn't have your number. It's a cluster-fuck that's for sure. I can't imagine how I'd feel if I was in his position. I know how bad it was seeing you in that hospital bed in York." I can feel him shudder at the memory. He'd had to watch me being pushed in front of a train at York Station and then after that hear the news that as a result of my injuries we'd lost the baby we hadn't known we were expecting. They were very dark days for us, but we've overcome the past and have a bright future to look forward to, not just the baby we're having but our upcoming wedding as well. I glance at the engagement ring sparkling on my finger and remind myself for the hundredth time today how lucky I am.

"How on earth do I tell Teresa?" I remember she wasn't Sue's biggest fan back then, they've only developed a better relationship since Teresa had her son, but of course Sue won't remember him either. This is so complicated. "Will Sue even know who I am?"

"Let's talk to Prez first, he may have a better idea of how to handle Teresa," Angel suggests. I want to laugh as Prez is the only one of us who seems able to temper Teresa's fiery temper. We've all been on the receiving end of it at some point, but he's normally the target for her fury more than anyone else. Their's is definitely a passionate relationship, one minute they're fighting and the next they're having amazing make up sex. Angel and I have a much calmer albeit no less passionate life. Who would have guessed that little girl from York would end up living halfway across the world with a bunch of bikers, not me, that's for certain.

Angel's hand is caressing my bump whilst he continues to hold me close. I place my hand on top of his, so grateful that after the grief of the past, we have this second chance. I know Jackson bitterly regrets splitting with Sue and was desperate for her to wake up so he could have his second chance, the question is now, will he ever get that? I hope he does. Angel and I almost didn't make it when I fled home to England, leaving him behind, convinced that he was better off without me. I couldn't have been more wrong as he quickly followed me to bring me back, but the danger I thought I'd left behind was already waiting for me in England when I returned and I almost died, again! It wasn't the last time either, the evil followed us back here, but touch wood, we're in a good place now.

I know Hellion MC have had a rough time of things as well, but thanks to Sue there's now a relationship between the two clubs. They're working together now to find out who did this to Sue and to stop them hurting anyone else. I'm not naive enough to believe that this will be easy or without some cost to us, but I know both Hellion and Severed cannot sit back and let evil succeed.

I think back to just a few months ago when my friends from England came over and spent some time with us in amongst their tour dates. I don't think Angel was overly happy to find out my friend was a male stripper, but it did make for an entertaining evening when Alex and his fellow strippers taught the guys from Severed and Hellion how to dance. I can see Sue sat there, clear as day, laughing her head off and that's a great memory, just tempered by the sadness of her accident and this further news. I suppose the positive here is that she's woken up and she's going to be okay. It was a horrific accident, and we were lucky not to lose her.

I return my focus to Angel and the question of how we break the news to Teresa. "Have you seen her today? I missed her this morning so I'm not quite sure what mood she was in?

"Considering the language she was using to Prez I think maybe we should hang fire till we've spoken to him," Angel laughs. "In fact, I think we delegate to him and then you can sort out with the others who goes to visit Sue and when."

None of the guys at the MC are cowards, but they're definitely wary of Teresa when she's going off on one of her rants.

"I think that sounds like a plan." I agree.

Business settled, Angel leans over and kisses me. "Now we've got that sorted I think you and I need to go lay down for a rest." He suggests.

I 'm about to protest that I'm not tired and need him to stop treating me like a fragile flower when I recognize the look of lust in his eyes. "Oh, I think that's a very good idea indeed." I've barely finished replying before Angel stands up with me in his arms and starts carrying me to our room at the clubhouse.

Did I say I like my new life? I don't, I bloody love it!

CHAPTER TWENTY ONE

Jackson

We're sitting in Church bemoaning the lack of activity from Carnal when several of our phones vibrate with an incoming message. Swiping the screen, I see it's from Smokey and am almost ready to ignore it till the meeting has finished when I spot the word missing. Scanning the message I'm instantly on my feet as are several of the Hellion crew.

"What's up?" Declan queries. I show him my phone,

Help! Shelby is missing, her mom's just called in a panic. Do you have eyes on her?"

"Shit! Shelby's missing." I shout out. "Who's on watch?"

"We're not watching the girl, we've been watching the creep. That's what you asked us to do. He's not been near her for the last two days." Cowboy tells the room.

Too late I understand that we should have been watching Shelby too, but the focus had been on his interaction with Carnal and trying to find who was funding the trafficking. Could this explain the lack of activity with him, Carnal are still focused on obtaining the girls they were wanting to transport. It's a stupid error and I should have known better. I don't have time to beat myself up over this right now, the focus has to be on finding Shelby.

Several of the guys are already on their phones, checking in and trying to find anyone who might know when and where she was taken. I try to call Smokey, but the lines engaged so I leave a voicemail asking her to call me straight back. It's only five minutes before she does but it feels like an eternity.

Smokey's sobbing when I answer. "Jackson, he's got them both!" Her words run together after that, intelligible, and I have to ask her to repeat herself. I put my phone on speaker so everyone can hear, and the room falls silent.

"Shelby's mom called me as she'd had a call from the school to say Shelby didn't turn up this morning and they hadn't been notified of any absence. Shelby had left for school as normal along with her little sister, Emma, who she drops off on the way at the primary school. There was no reason to think she wasn't going to school, she had her uniform on and they'd both taken their backpacks. When her mom checked in with the kindergarten her little sister hadn't turned up either." There are various obscenities muttered around the room at this news. "Please tell me he hasn't got those beautiful girls?" Smokey starts crying again.

"We had eyes on him rather than the girls, but he hasn't been near them for the last couple of days," I confirm. "Can you get her mom and bring her to the clubhouse, Declan and his team and the guys from Severed are here and we need to find out what she knows so we can work out where to start?"

"Give me forty-five minutes, we'll be there." Smokey hangs up before I can say anything else. I turn to look at Declan, hoping he has some advice on where we go from here.

"Do we know the address of her home and the schools so we can look at the routes?" He's already got a laptop out and opened some mapping software. "If we know which way they headed we can try and access some CCTV feeds in the area and track her movements that way?"

One of the guys who's been watching the creep quickly gives Declan the information and Cam starts typing on the laptop. "Damn, there's really limited coverage in that area," he mutters. His fingers are flying over the keys. "What time did she set off?" He looks around the room for answers.

"She leaves home around 7:45 and walks her little sister to the preschool club, gets her there for around 8:00 then walks over to her own bus stop on Chapel Street to catch the bus to Castlemaine which leaves around 8:30." A voice calls out.

"The high school in Castlemaine installed CCTV last year, I remember there being a stink about it from some of the parents," I mention. "Declan, any chance you can get into their system and see if we can see anyone hanging around the high school as well?"

Declan quickly keys something into his phone, a moment later his phone sounds a text message and once he's read it he confirms that it's sorted, we'll have all the feeds we asked for soon.

There's plenty of activity in the room already as several of the guys are studying the intel for the past week, trying to spot any kind of pattern or clues that might help us locate the girls. We have a plasma screen on the wall and it's currently scrolling through a feed of the surveillance photos we've taken. Something catches my eye but before I can work out what it was the image has moved on. It can't have been important and I'm sure it will come back to me.

When the school surveillance comes through we're disappointed to see that Shelby didn't get off the bus, we've not been able to confirm yet that she got on it in the first place so whilst its negative news it does help us narrow the search field both in terms of distance and time.

Shelby's mom arrives soon after and as you'd expect looks absolutely distraught. She's so worried for her girls. Shelby had confided in her about her fear she was being followed, thanks to Smokey's earlier intervention there's been a lot more open communication between Shelby and her mother. Both sides trying to be honest with each other rather than keeping things bottled up.

"I can't believe I ever got involved with that creep," she sobs. "Or that my poor girl ever thought I'd choose to believe him rather than her." Smokey pulls her into a hug, trying to comfort her.

"You're a good mom, don't ever doubt that, but sadly, not all moms are, and Shelby will see that every day at school and at the ranch. You work so hard for your girls to give them a good life, you sacrifice for them. Some moms barely even remember they have kids."

Smokey's right. It burns me that Shelby needs to be at the ranch when she has a mom who obviously loves and cares for her but doesn't get to spend enough time with her because she has to work two jobs just to keep a roof over their heads. When this is all over I need to have a word with Rebel and see if there isn't some way we can help out Shelby's mom with a job at the ranch that would mean she could spend more time with her girls and still afford to live.

The morning passes slowly, the only news being leads that have been exhausted. Whoever took Shelby and her little sister made sure they did it out of sight of cameras that's for sure.

Frustrated at the lack of news a few of us decide to head out and check out the possible routes that could have been taken, we've all got a map of the camera locations that

Declan sent to our phones, so we know where has already been searched.

The creep still hasn't left home, probably sleeping off last night's hangover, but we agree to double the watch we already have on him just in case he is involved somehow and can lead us to a clue.

Pausing on our way out I reassure Shelby's mom that we will find her girls. I can't help hoping that I'm not making false promises.

CHAPTER TWENTY TWO

Rebel

Chris has been quiet and withdrawn since the night Jackson came over and I'm not sure how best to support him. I know he has a lot on his mind and has taken hope that Declan may be able to come up with a solution for him that will help assuage the guilt he feels. I know he wants to spend more time with me, I want that too, but I also understand his need to put right all the wrongs his father perpetrated. Chris is a good guy at heart, unlike that evil scumbag who was his sperm donor. As much as I hate seeing Chris struggling, it has taken the pressure off for me, it's been easier to hide my own concerns from him. There isn't a day goes by that I don't think about the possibility of Aaron being my genetic Dad. For someone who never wanted to know, suddenly it's all I can think about.

The girls decided that we'd wait till Christmas to do the DNA tests, that way I could buy them for everyone as gifts, they still don't suspect that I have any interest in this other than helping them find out a few things about their genetic traits and helping Maeve trace her own father. Waiting for those few months almost kills me some days but provides relief on others.

It's strange that we all had some form of dysfunctional childhood, but we all survived and became stronger for it. We were the lucky ones, I know that. Even Chris fits that pattern. Aside from Maeve, we all grew up surrounded by love, even if it wasn't from our own parent, Eve found hers with Teresa's family. Is that why so many of us are passionate about the ranch and what it can do for the kids who go there?

What will I do with the knowledge once I have it, it's not just myself that I need to consider as this affects other lives as well. I have to be conscious and sensitive of that.

I try and put my concerns aside for a moment and think of someone else. There's so much happening around me right now it's hard to decide who needs me first.

Jackson's in pain knowing Sue can't remember him, Chris is hurting because he's a good man faced with an incredibly difficult task, and the people around me are hurting because they're concerned both for Sue and about the horrors that could be happening on our doorstep, the trafficking.

When I look back on my life, as dysfunctional as it was, to me it was normal and perfect. It's only society who thought it was wrong because I wasn't brought up in a typical family environment. What's typical these days? Surely it's more important that a child is brought up by someone who will love and nurture them rather than someone who fits a so-called societal norm. It's much worse for a child to be brought up in a home without love, in a life filled with neglect and abuse. What's a parent at the end of the day? Surely it's the person who raised you and loved you and cared for you? Does a genetic match make a person more qualified to be a parent?

Chris knocks on the office door and walks in, a look of concern on his face, the phone still in his hand.

"What's wrong?" I ask, worried.

"Shelby and her little sister are missing," He pulls me into a hug, somehow knowing that's just what I need.

"What can we do to help?"

"I knew you'd say that" he responds, "I told them we'd be right over to help with the search."

With that he hands me my coat I hadn't noticed he was holding and grabbing my purse on the way out we head straight for his car.

CHAPTER TWENTY THREE

Jackson

I put my phone back in my pocket. That was Eve. True to her word, she has been arranging for visitors from Severed to visit Sue, although no one has had the heart to tell her about Elvis yet. Whenever she asks where he is they just tell her that Teresa will be visiting soon.

Teresa is struggling with what's happened and hasn't been able to bring herself to actually visit Sue, although from what Eve tells me, Teresa's there in the visitor room every day regardless. Sue can't stay awake for any length of time and while she's sleeping there are still people there talking to her about the good old days, much like when Rebel, Smokey and the girls were sat with her every day whilst she was in her coma.

Eve's going to visit with her this afternoon and we're both a little scared how Sue will react to that, as she only met Eve just before Elvis was killed. She's been fine with the visitors she's had so far and known who they all were, but it's hard to gauge just how far back in time her memory has taken her. This will be a good test of it. Teresa's waiting to see what happens with that visit. I get it, reliving that period in her life will be incredibly painful for her.

I've headed out with a number of my brothers to see if I can find any sign of Shelby and her little sister. Her mom was able to give us a recent picture of the girls in their school uniforms and we're going to go door to door along the routes we identified earlier. I don't get it. The only camera footage we've got with them in it doesn't show anyone else, no suspicious vehicles, nothing out of the ordinary that we haven't been able to explain. It doesn't make sense.

The street I'm currently riding down leads to a dead end. So far no one I've spoken to has seen anything, that said a lot of people aren't at home at this time of day so we may need to repeat this exercise later this evening when they're back from work.

The old house at the end of the block is for sale and looks like it hasn't been lived in for some time now. The windows and door are all boarded up, but I get a sense that something is off. I stop the bike and park up. Without getting off the bike I look around first, trying to work out what triggered the feeling. Nothing is immediately apparent, but I decide to take a closer look.

It looks like this was once a well looked after home, the shape of the garden beds showing that someone took pride in the garden, a pretty little fence running along the front of the property although the paint has peeled in a number of places. The gate isn't shut and there's enough room to pass by without opening it fully as I walk through. I catch something move out of the corner of my eye and my hand immediately goes to the gun I have in the back of my jeans, but I relax my grip when I recognize it's just a cat, a stray from the state of its matted coat.

Looking ahead of me once more the front of the house doesn't look like it's been disturbed, the boards are still nailed in place. There's an unnatural sense of quiet and abandonment about the place the closer I get. The garden is overgrown but the path around to the back of the property is still passable. A little love and attention and this could be a lovely home again for someone. The back of the property is enclosed by a high fence, and I can see a few fruit trees still bearing fruit at the back. A couple of rocking chairs still sit out on the deck as though just awaiting their owner to come home and relax there.

As I get closer to the back of the house I notice the dust on the deck has been disturbed near the door, and if I'm not mistaken, although the door looks to be boarded up, it's been opened recently. I debate calling it in, but don't want to look stupid when in all likelihood it's just going to be a homeless person looking for some shelter for the night.

The door opens much more quietly than I expected, as though the hinges have been recently oiled. Dust motes fly around the kitchen, disturbed by my entrance, visible in the tiny cracks of light passing through the holes in the boards on the windows.

Someone elderly must have lived here judging by the decor that I can see and the lack of modern appliances. An old range lies dark and dormant against one wall, and the sink sits under the window. I'm not sure if the door to the side of me leads to a basement or a pantry but the one ahead looks to lead to a hallway.

I choose the door to my side and discover it is indeed an old pantry, a heavy stone slab against one wall with tiers of shelves above in a u shape, hugging each wall. There's still food in here, cans of all descriptions covered in a fine layer of dust, alongside plates and bowls. It reminds me of my grans kitchen when I was little. A happy memory. There's a circle without dust where a can should have been. It looks like it was recently removed. Another indication that I'm probably going to encounter someone homeless in one of the rooms.

Walking out of the pantry back into the kitchen I glance around looking for any sign of the empty can. There's nothing obvious. Would a homeless person clean up after themselves? Would a child trafficker? Who knows. I can't say I have experience of either.

The hallway is dark, no light getting in from the boarded-up windows, so I use the torch on my phone to see where I'm going, almost dropping it when I see the small foot-print that has disturbed the layer of dust on the floor.

Not wanting to disturb whoever is on the other side of the door I send a text alerting the guys to what I have found, and make sure my phone is on silent, so any response won't be heard.

What do I do now? How many men are in there with them? Should I risk going in alone. The room can't be that big based on the size of the house. Have they already heard me? I haven't been noisy, but I am in my biker boots, and they do sound against the wooden floor.

I pause a moment, trying to hear anything on the other side. There's nothing. What did I expect? That the bad guys would be audibly announcing their presence for me? There's no sound of anyone moving, no conversation, no heavy breathing. The phone hasn't vibrated a response to my message yet, so I don't know if any back up is even on the way.

That's when I hear it, a creaking floorboard followed by a young child's choked back sob. That makes my mind up for me, I can't wait any longer, I'm going in. I draw my gun and ready myself. Facing the door, I kick it open, gun ahead of me and freeze when I see the sight in front of me. What the hell have I just walked into.

CHAPTER TWENTY FOUR

Rebel

I put the phone down and feel a flood of relief. "Chris, they've found her, they're heading back to the clubhouse now." I shout over. We're searching the back of the gardens on one of the streets where they back up to the woods. We've looked so many places now I can't remember the name of this particular one.

Jackson just told me that he'd found them both safe and that he'd fill us in when we get back to the clubhouse. It's not what we thought apparently. Now color me intrigued.

"Will Declan be at the clubhouse do you know?" Chris asks as he taps his fingers unconsciously against the steering wheel in tune with the music whilst we're stopped at a red light.

"I'm not sure, I know he was involved in the search, but I

don't know if he was actually there or somewhere else checking video feeds, why?" I respond.

"If he's there I might ask him if we can have a chat when all this stuff is over, I don't want to distract him from what he's working on for Jackson and the guys." Just saying the words seems to lift a visible weight off his shoulders.

"Sounds good to me. If he's not there today I'm sure he will be soon." I place my hand on his thigh and caress it gently, hoping to show my support. Chris reaches down and squeezes my hand in his just as the lights change, quickly returning it to the steering wheel as we turn off in the direction of the clubhouse.

"Wonder what Jackson meant when he told us it wasn't what we thought?" I muse. Chris's response of 'No idea." makes me realize I'd voiced that out loud and not in my head. I need to be careful that none of my other confused thoughts become audible today. I'd hate to add to the fracas facing the club right now, especially with a bomb-shell about who my father might be.

Why does life have to be so complicated these days, up until my thirtieth birthday everything seemed to be so normal and since then I feel like I've been on a permanent roller coaster ride. Twists and turns, highs and lows nonstop.

Don't get me wrong, I'm not unhappy with my life but a little less excitement would be good, well less of the trau-matic excitement that is.

During the drive my thoughts don't turn far from the DNA idea, it's always there just under the surface waiting to surprise me, but today I'm thinking more about Maeve and the contrast between our lives. I was so lucky to be taken in by the club, but I know that Maeve was passed from pillar to post and most of it wasn't good. She won't go into detail, but I suspect that the last foster family had a dad who got a little too handsy with her, hence her ending up back in the home.

When she talks about the home there's no mention of affection for or from any of the staff. It sounds like a cold environment to raise a child in. They'd taken care of her physical needs, they'd fed and clothed her and given her a bed to sleep, made sure she was enrolled in school but there doesn't seem to have been any of the affection or recognition that a child needs and thrives on. No one attended her sports days, her parent/teacher meetings. I wonder if they even bothered reading her report card. Did she get treats when she'd done well, a talking to when she could have improved? Did she ever get a hug?

Thinking back, I cannot imagine what my life would have looked like, would have felt like, without those things and all along I just took them for granted.

Maeve helps out at the ranch as much as her crappy job allows but I can't help feeling we need to do something more for her, to make her feel more a part of our family since she doesn't have one of her own. I wonder if we could create a job for her at the ranch, then stop myself.

The ranch isn't big enough to give all these women jobs, it's doing okay at the moment but maybe I need to start looking for some investors to increase what we offer.

There's so much I'd like to do with the kids, more fun stuff, but for now the focus has just been on keeping them safe and teaching them some life skills. When this is all over I guess Chris isn't the only one who needs to sit down and talk through his problems. I should really sit down and talk with Jackson and Dee Dee about the ranch and how we can move it on to the next level. I'm brim full of ideas but don't have the bank balance to make any of them come true.

Chris doesn't speak for the rest of the journey to the club-house, but I'm not concerned as I can hear him mumbling along to the music on the stereo. I can see he's a little less stressed and that makes me feel much better. I've been so worried for him. I smile every time I recognize where he's got the lyrics wrong. Jackson had messaged me a link to a YouTube video of Peter Kay, a Brit comedian who did a sketch on misheard song lyrics and it was so funny, and so right! There have been plenty of times I've misheard song lyrics and it's only when I see the lyrics on my Amazon music channel that I grasp how wrong I was.

Some nights when Chris is away I just sit and read on my Kindle, with Amazon Music on the TV. Occasionally I'll look up and find myself getting lost in the lyrics of the song. I guess it shows that when we listen to music we never fully hear it, we have to see the words written down to fully understand them.

I guess that's a bit like the people around us, we're all so busy these days that we listen but do we really hear what's being said? Maybe if we'd really listened to Shelby we wouldn't have had this scare today. We're so lucky that Smokey did recognize something was wrong in the past and made the effort to sit and really listen to her, then acted on it. If she hadn't it doesn't bear thinking about, today would have had a very different outcome. She might not have even made it to today. Again, it's something else I think we need to really consider for the ranch, making sure that the right people are in place both to listen to the kids but also people who the kids feel comfortable unburdening themselves to.

I kind of feel that kids today have it so much harder than when I was their age. I know everyone struggles more financially, but today's kids have the added burden of social media, more is expected of them both educationally and socially. Kids can be so mean when someone doesn't have the most expensive sneakers, the latest phone or expensive clothes. Today everything is about putting on a fake persona, growing up too quickly.

Looking back, I was a spoiled princess. I was surrounded by love, rules and pretty much always received what I asked for. Sometimes I had to work for what I wanted but then it was more rewarding when I got it because I knew I'd earned it. That said my definition of work was pretty easy, it might have been polishing one of the bikes or getting a certain grade on my test or essay whereas I see so many teens now having to work after school just to contribute to the family expenses with very little left over for them for a treat.

I'm pulled from my melancholy thoughts as we drive through the clubhouse gates. I'm home, this will and always has been my safe place.

CHAPTER TWENTY FIVE

Jackson

E nding the call with Rebel, I turn back to the scene in front of me. I've already spoken to the clubhouse. They haven't moved from where they're sitting for either of the calls.

Shelby and her little sister, Emma, are huddled together on the tattered sofa, and they've confirmed that no one else is in the house. In fact, no one else is involved. This was all Shelby's doing. I feel relief that it wasn't what we feared but anger at the distress this has caused her mother.

Using the usual childhood logic, Shelby thought she was doing the right thing. She hadn't known that we'd had people watching the creep rather than her and was scared that if he couldn't get to her he'd go for her little sister instead.

"Come on you guys, let's get you somewhere safe and get a decent meal in you." I look at the remains of the baked bean tins on the coffee table. That's what they'd been eating, cold baked beans and dry bread along with a bottle of lukewarm water to drink.

I don't bother investigating the rest of the house, I don't really want to see what squalor she thought was better to live in so that she could keep her sister safe. I just want to get these girls back to their terrified mother. At least she knows they're safe now and has spoken to them both briefly, just to reassure herself that they're okay.

I gather up the few things that aren't still in Shelby's back-pack and hand them to her. "Anything else?" I check.

Shelby shakes her head.

"Right then, let's get you back to your mom, she's worried sick about the pair of you." I try to keep my voice friendly and jovial, but Emma looks as if she's about to bawl.

"Will Shelby and me be in trouble?" her lip tremors.

"No darlin', you're not in trouble, everyone's just glad you're okay, but we do need to talk to Shelby some, just to work out what scared her so much she thought this was a good idea and to make sure she doesn't need to get that scared again."

She's standing so close to Shelby you'd need a can opener to separate them, her tiny arms gripped so tightly to her sister's leg her fingers are almost white.

"It's okay sweet pea," Shelby reassures her. "Bet Mom will be glad to see you won't she?"

I hadn't noticed just how stuffy and dusty the house was till we were back outside and breathing in the fresh air.

"Why this place?" I gesture back at the house.

"I knew it was empty, no one comes here, not even to tend the garden. It felt safe, overlooked if you know what I mean. People walk past it and just ignore it." Shelby tries to explain.

"Yep, I know what you mean darlin', I would have walked past it myself if I hadn't been looking for you. Right, hop in." I open the door of the SUV I asked for when I called the clubhouse to let them know I'd found the girls. I'm about to get on my bike to follow them back when the prospect gets out and calls me over.

"They want you to drive em back, boss. I don't think they feel safe with a strange face." He looks crestfallen, I guess he's saddened that the girls are scared of him. I don't really want anyone else on my bike, but I also don't want to leave it here unattended any longer than needed so I shrug my shoulders and swap keys with him,

I've barely started the engine when a little voice pops up from behind.

"Can we get a milkshake on the way please? I want a milk-shake." Shelby tries to hush her sister, but the little girl is adamant she wants one. I'm not surprised after being in that hellhole.

"It's okay," I reassure them both. "We can go via the diner and get you both a milkshake."

Emma's face lights up but Shelby's face drops.

"Thanks, but we don't have enough money for milkshakes. We'll just head straight back." She turns to her sister then and continues. "You know we can't afford milkshakes sweet pea, that's just for birthdays and treats."

The look of disappointment on that little girls face breaks my heart over something so simple as a milkshake, but the stubborn pride emanating from Shelby makes me think my next words very carefully.

"Would you ladies do me the honor of letting me buy you a milkshake on the way back? I feel like I deserve a treat for finding you safe and it would be very rude of me to only get one for myself." I suggest.

I can tell that Shelby's pride still wants to say no, but I've given her an out here and after a moments pause she gracefully accepts my offer, its accompanied by a whoop of joy from Emma.

It's only a short detour to the diner and we order the drinks to takeout as I'm very aware their mom is probably pacing holes in the floor back at the clubhouse waiting to see her girls. I almost don't order one for myself until Shelby reminds me that's the whole reason we're here, I wanted to treat myself.

I can't remember the last time I had a milkshake, it was probably when Rebel was little, and it takes me a while to choose but not as long as Emma. She takes what seems like forever but finally settles on banana.

I'm relieved to be back in the car and on the road.

We've barely made it through the clubhouse gates when a figure comes running towards the car from the front door. I have to disengage the locks on the doors before I cut the engine as I can hear their mom frantically trying to open the door. Before the engine dies she's managed to get both her girls out of the car and is on her knees on the ground, her arms wrapped around them, holding them so tightly to her they must be hurting and she's bawling so loudly she can barely get her words out. I recognize the odd one such as babies and safe.

We must wait there for a good ten minutes before she starts to pull herself together. I'm so relieved for her that today has had a happy ending.

I watch them for a while longer, still hugging, all crying happy tears. I want to give them this moment, this time just to be together. To feel the love.

"I hate to disturb you ladies, but do you think we could take this inside now? My old bones could do with a seat." Shelby starts to look a little alarmed.

"Don't worry darlin', no one's in trouble. We'll give you some time to just get yourselves settled but if you don't mind, we would like a chat with you later. Just to find out what made you so scared you felt you needed to run away and to see what we can do to help you feel safer."

"You're not cross with me?" She looks between me and her mom.

"Darlin', we're all just so relieved you're safe and glad you're back with your mom." I reassure her.

Satisfied she's not in trouble Shelby starts to lead the way into the clubhouse, her shoulders and back straight and confident, never letting go of Emma's hand the whole time.

CHAPTER TWENTY SIX

Jackson

The clubhouse is quiet when we walk in, I'm guessing the old ladies have arranged to keep everyone out of the way, so we don't spook Shelby and Emma. I know they're scared but we need some answers from them. We need to go about this carefully.

Rebel walks out from the kitchen and the noise of the swinging door is enough to cause a reaction. Emma huddles closer to Shelby, her hand tightening against her sisters to the point I can see Shelby's hand go white.

"Hey, Shelby and Emma, so good to see you guys safe!" Rebel calls across the room. "Thought you could maybe do with a snack or two." That said she raises her hands in front of her and they're overflowing with fries, cookies, popcorn and all kinds of sugary crap. It does the trick though and Emma loosens her grip a little as a wide smile fills her face.

Rebel gestures to a table against the wall that has a large bench seat around it and we all head over. Shelby's mom carefully sits next to Emma, close enough to feel the heat from her leg but not close enough to startle her.

"Do you girls mind if a couple of my friends join us while you tell us what's been happening?" I ask.

"Do we have to talk about it? Can't we just leave it alone now you've found us?" Shelby pleads.

"I'm sorry darlin', what you share with us could help save some other young girls, you do understand that don't you?" I try to reason with her.

Shelby casts her eyes down, examining the table so closely I almost feel like she's seeing straight through it. "I guess." She pauses, pulling her sister in closer and hugging her tight. "I'm sorry,' she has started to cry, a single tear tracking its way down her face. "I didn't want to worry anyone, but I needed to keep Emma safe."

"That's all we want too darlin', to keep you girls safe." I reassure her. "We're just going to wait a moment or two for my friends to join us then you can tell us all what happened."

Shelby nods her head slowly, and Rebel reaches over to place her hand on hers, offering reassurance.

"You've nothing to be scared of here, I promise you. These guys are going to protect you, you know them from the ranch, remember?"

Just then the front door bangs open and both girls scream out in fear. I turn, my hand on my gun ready to stop whoever it is.

"Shelby!" Smokey cries out, running towards us. "I'm so glad you're safe."

"For fucks sake woman, I almost shot you!" I shout at her. Smokey barely breaks her stride when I rebuke her, too concerned for the girl in front of her. "Not to mention you scared the crap out of them both." I gesture at the two girls and Smokey stalls and looks heartbroken.

"Oh girls, I'm so sorry. The last thing I want to do is scare you." She wrings her hands.

"Never mind, just come sit down. The others will be here in a minute. You might as well hear what they have to say." I gesture at the seat next to Rebel, ensuring that the empty seats for my brothers all face the door.

Smokey is fussing over the girls whilst their mom just seems to sit there, shell shocked, she looks like she still can't quite believe her girls are there in front of her. I can't imagine the hell she must have been through this morning.

There's a knock at the front door then it opens, Declan and Cam leading the way, Aaron behind them.

"Shelby, Emma, these are my friends. They're here to help. Can you tell us what happened to you today and why you were at that house?" I introduce them to her, hoping that what she tells us isn't going to be more bad news.

"I'm sorry I caused so much trouble," Shelby starts then falters. Her shoulders shake with her crying, and she needs a moment and a hug from her mom before she's ready to continue.

"He'd started watching Emma, not just me," she pauses and reaches out for her sister's hand. "He was there every morning when I took her to school, and I got scared."

"Did he hurt either of you?" Declan questions. I think we're all holding our breath waiting on her answer and it's a massive relief when she answers in the negative.

"No, but I knew he would. That's why I had to get us out of there, I had to keep Emma safe Mom, I'm so sorry." Her mom reaches over and takes her hand, holding it tightly.

"I'm just so glad to have you both back safely, Shelby, but promise me you'll never do anything crazy like that again."

Shelby lowers her eyes to the table and hesitates. "I can't promise that I won't do everything in my power to keep Emma safe, I'm sorry."

"Shelby," I get her attention. "Do you think you could promise that you'll come to me or one of my club brothers if you ever feel like you're in danger again? Would that be a fair request?"

Shelby looks around the table and seems to consider my suggestion for a moment or two. "Yeah, I think I could promise that."

"Thank God," her mom utters., her grip tightening on Shelby's hand. "Thank you. You scared the life out of me this morning, I thought he'd taken you."

"So, tell us what happened, how long had you been planning this?" I start the questioning as gently as I can, I don't want her to feel intimidated or that she's being interrogated.

"I hadn't been planning it really, it was an idea in the back of my mind until last night when I saw him outside. That's when I knew I had to do something. I knew about the empty house and thought we could hide there for a few days. Hopefully if he couldn't find us he'd go somewhere else, look for someone else." Shelby looks horrified by what she just uttered. "I didn't want him to hurt anyone else, honest, but I hoped that if he found someone else they'd have someone watching out for them, protecting them and that they'd stop him. He's not a nice man."

"Did he ever hurt you, Shelby?" It's a question I wish to hell I didn't have to ask and am so relieved when she says no.

"He didn't but I knew he was going to, I know Mom told him to go away and leave us alone, but he never really went away. He was always hanging around outside when Mom was at work, and he could tell I knew he was there. He'd give me this knowing smirk, it made my skin crawl. I figured whilst he was just watching me I could handle it, but when he started watching Emma the way he used to look at me, I just knew."

"Why that house?" I'm curious.

"Because he'd never been around there as far as I know, it was somewhere overlooked. I figured at least there'd be a bed for Emma. I didn't have time to plan it though, I was going to sneak out some blankets and a couple of her toys and some decent food, but I had to adapt and get what I could before I left this morning as Mom was still at home."

"I'm just glad you're both safe." Shelby's mom is still holding on to both of her girls. It's like she's scared to let them go. "Can we go home now?" She turns and addresses me.

"No!" Shelby cries out. "He's still out there. He's still a risk."

She's right, just because we found her and her sister safe this time, whilst he's still out there they are both at risk.

"Why don't you all come stay at the ranch for a few days?" Smokey suggests. "It will give your mom a bit of peace of mind, and we can speak to your school and get some homework set so you don't fall behind? How does that sound?"

Shelby looks to her mom for approval, I know she feels safe at the ranch, and we can probably protect her better there than her house right now.

Declan has been quiet until now but adds his opinion. "I think that's a good idea. We'll make sure you're safe, Shelby, you can trust us to keep you and Emma safe and to make sure this guy can't hurt you." There's a quiet confidence in Declan's voice and I suspect his solution to this guy might be a little more permanent than I'd have come up with.

"Thank you for your kind offer, I really appreciate everything you've already done for us, but I can't ask you to do more," Shelby's mom declares.

"Let me stop you right there!" Smokey interrupts. "I know what you're going to say, and you are not a bother and it's not a problem." She reassures her. "You'd be doing me a massive favor as I'm not going to be able to sleep unless I know your girls are safe." Smokey's tone leaves no room for disagreement and it's quickly agreed that we'll stop by their house and pick up some personal stuff and then take all three of them to the ranch until things settle down.

I'm relieved. Today could have turned out so much worse than it has. That creep is still out there and a risk to the girls, and possibly others. Looking at Declan I don't think that's going to be an issue for too much longer.

CHAPTER TWENTY SEVEN

Rebel

I'm back at the ranch as Jackson asked me to get a couple of rooms ready so that Shelby, Emma and their mom can stay for a few days till they come up with a solution for the creep. I'm just glad they found them both safe and well.

"Hey, Danni, can you give me a hand making up some rooms?" I call over to her. Danni is a regular volunteer here at the ranch, despite having five kids of her own. Her green hair makes her unmissable at the ranch, it was the most amazing shade of blue the other month and I must admit I do get a bit of hair envy every now and then.

Danni is always such a help whenever she volunteers, especially with the horse riding but she hates camping and you've not seen anything till you've seen her running from a spider or other creepy crawly when they occasionally show up in the barn.

As we make the beds we chat about her kids, she was a young mom, only 16 when she had her first, but she's done a great job of raising them. She's got an eleven-year-old, an eight year old, six year old twins and a new baby. She's a natural with the kids at the ranch, knowing what it's like to be on your own and have to fight for everything. Her parents are really religious and turned their back on her because they didn't approve of her life choices. Just because she doesn't go to church every Sunday doesn't make her a bad person, nor do her tattoos or being an unmarried mother. She's a supportive mother not just to her own kids but the kids she cares for here at the ranch as well. I mean she loves Dolly Parton for god's sake, how can anyone who loves Dolly Parton be bad!

Danni tells me she's about to get a couple of new tattoos, one is a six colored rose with her kids names on it and then a Phoenix on her left shoulder. She's been showing me the pictures of what she has planned, and I love them. I'm tempted to get a new tattoo but still undecided over what I want and where.

Before we leave the room Danni places a few crystals around. "They're for calm and protection." She advises when she sees me watching her. I look at the tattoo of a pentagram on her ankle and smile. Another reason her parents disowned her is that she's part of a coven but they're not spooky witches like you'd find in Hocus Pocus, it's a coven who work with herbs and crystals to balance Chakra and enlightenment. I admit I don't know if I believe in all that, but she has such a lovely outlook on life I find it hard to disregard her beliefs.

She's only a few years younger than me and I often find I'm comparing myself to her. Here she is at 27 with five kids and I've not even started a family yet. For a moment I lose myself in an image of Jackson holding a grandchild and my heart melts.

Danni had dropped out of a beauty course when she had her eldest but still uses what she learned to do the odd pamper session for some of the girls occasionally and readily agrees to come back tomorrow and do a session for Shelby, Emma and their mom. I'm sure it will help them feel better and a little more settled.

"Great job," I congratulate us when both rooms are freshened up and ready for our visitors. "How about some brownie cookie dough and a vanilla latte before you head off home? I think we deserve a treat and they're not going to get here for at least another half hour.

"Two of my favorite things, you got me!' Danni readily agrees.

"You okay for time or do you need to get back for the kids?" I offer.

"It's fine, the boys are both at home so can take care of them." I smile at Danni's description of her two live in partners. Her living situation is like something out of one of the books she reads and shares with me. She had two boyfriends, liked them both and didn't want to choose between them, and luckily for her they were fine with that, and they all live together. It works really well for them all. I'm not sure if her parents know about her living situation but can just imagine the apoplexy that would cause them.

For Christian people they sure are unchristian in the way they've treated their daughter and grandkids. Still, their loss is our gain, and we're delighted to have her help out when she can.

As we enter the kitchen I can hear that Dee Dee has already put on Danni's playlist as we call it. It's a mix of Dolly, Carrie Underwood, Keith Urban and Tim McGraw. Sure, enough there's brownie cookie dough on the counter, a vanilla latte for Danni and a chai tea for me. Dee Dee has a special place in her heart for Danni and I love that.

"How are my babies?" Dee Dee greets Danni with a hug and before long Danni has her phone out showing off photos of her kids and answering Dee Dee's hundred and one questions.

"Should I be jealous?" I call to Dee Dee as she oohs and ahhs over yet another baby photo, my mouth half full of cookie dough.

"No, not jealous, but you really should have made me a grandma by now." Dee Dee retorts.

I groan out loud. "Not this again!"

Danni, the traitor, just laughs.

"So now you've had your fix of photo's why not tell me what the story is about Shelby and why she needs to stay here?" Danni knows the ranch is more of a day retreat and the kids go home each night, even though we're seriously considering enlarging our offering with short respite stays. It's still only in the thinking about stage though.

We fill her in on what's been happening to Shelby and her face falls. "That poor kid. Will they be okay?"

"Yeah, they're coming here for a few days and Smokey's going to be here with them. Jackson and the guys are searching for him and will let us know when it's safe for them to go home."

"That'll be good for Smokey, she needs something to keep her distracted aside from visiting James at the hospital all the time." Danni nods. "Can we include Smokey in the pamper session tomorrow? I think she'd enjoy it as well." Danni offers.

"Oh, that sounds like a great idea, any chance I can join in as well?" Dee Dee grins.

"I'm not sure Danni has enough magic in her beauty kit to handle you old woman," I laugh. Dee Dee looks fake affronted and that sets us all off laughing hysterically.

Despite the tense situation that led to the three of us sitting here I have to say it's been a real tonic for me. I needed something to distract me from all the questions running through my head constantly and my worries about Chris.

"Perfect timing!" I call out as Danni places her empty cup on the counter. I can hear the cars pulling up outside.

"Come on, let's go introduce you to your guinea pigs for tomorrow." I laugh in Danni's direction.

"Guinea pigs? Why you…" Danni play smacks my shoulder and pulls me in for a hug. "Good job I love you woman. Now lead the way…".

CHAPTER TWENTY EIGHT

Rebel

The girls and their Mum settled in fairly well last night, considering the stress they've all been through. Between Smokey, Dee Dee and Danni they soon started laughing, it's the best medicine and just what they need.

I've left them to enjoy their pamper session as I'm heading to the hospital to see Sue. Eve called me last night to let me know that she's been playing Sue some of her favorite music and showing her photos from Teresa's wedding and baby photos of her son Aaron Elvis. I can't believe that there are three Aaron's now, my possible dad, the president of Severed MC and his son. Talk about coincidence. Luckily everyone calls Teresa's husband Prez which makes it a little easier. Anyway, Sue seems to be recalling some memories here and there which has got to be a good thing.

The doctors had advised that after the traumatic injury and the coma that it may take weeks or months for Sue to regain her memory, but even that wasn't guaranteed. She could still suffer permanent memory loss, or maybe just not remember the moments just before and after the accident. It's different with everyone so we shouldn't get her hopes up.

Teresa has already had the most difficult conversation with her about losing Elvis. One of the things she remembered was Declan recovering her stolen ring, the one that Elvis had bought for her, so some of her post Elvis memories are there. Now that Sue knows about Elvis the doctor agreed it would be a good idea for her to have some visitors from the time her memory has lost, it might help her remember and it might help ease her grief.

I'm going to take in some photos from her time with us, but just group photos for now. They've suggested we don't tell her about her relationship with Jackson yet, she needs to recover more of her memories first or it could be too traumatic for her, and she'll just shut down again. Coming on the back of the news about Elvis it might be too much.

There are some great memories and the ones I'm really looking forward to sharing with her are the ones where we'd gone over to the Severed clubhouse to meet Eve's male stripper friends from England. That was one hell of a night, it's also the night Eve told Angel she was expecting his baby, at almost the same time he proposed to her. It feels like that was the last time everyone was truly happy, so much has happened in a short time to challenge that happiness.

As I enter the hospital room I'm pleased to see that Sue looks better than the last time I saw her. Don't get me wrong, she's still battered and bruised but she's sitting up, smiling and chatting with the nurse who is checking her vitals.

"Hello," she greets me, "I'm sorry, I think I recognize you, but I can't remember your name or where I know you from."

"Don't worry about it, I'm Rebel," I remind her. "I've come to keep you company and brought you some more photos to see if they help." The nurse finishes writing her findings on Sue's chart and bids us farewell.

I take the seat at the side of the bed and ask Sue what music she'd like on today. "I think I'd like some Shinedown, do I like Shinedown? Are they even a band?" She looks confused.

I grin wildly, knowing that it was me that introduced Sue to their music, and so very pleased that something from her time with us is still there for her. "Absolutely, you'd never heard of them when you first met me, but we played a lot of it at my thirtieth birthday party and you fell in love with them, almost as much as me."

I swap the CD in the player for her and set the volume to low so we can still hear each other talking.

"Did you say you brought some photos?" Sue looks at the bag I brought in with me with interest.

"Yep," I pull the album I compiled for her out of my bag and place it on the bed between us, ensuring that it's the right way up for Sue to turn the pages herself. "I'm going to leave this with you, so you can flip through it whenever you want."

Sue shifts slightly in the bed so she's in a better position to view the album but I don't miss the grimace of pain as she does.

"Don't worry," she reassures me, "it's slowly getting better. I've asked the doctor to reduce my pain meds as they were making me too woozy, and I want to start getting back to myself as soon as possible. The physio is coming by later to show me some more gentle exercises to help with the hurting." Knowing her so well I can tell some of the pain she's trying to hide isn't just physical, it's grief as well.

As she was talking she opened the album and gasped at the first image. It's a shot I captured of her on her own at one of our clubhouse get togethers and her head is thrown back in laughter. You can see her smile in her eyes and it's a beautiful shot of her. It's one of my personal favorites.

"Is that me?" She almost sounds surprised. I can see why though, she's currently a pale reflection of the woman in the picture. Her skin has lost its sun kissed complexion, her eyes are still bruised and her cheek swollen, not to mention the cuts, scrapes and bandages. "I look like I really loved life."

"You most certainly did, "I reassure her. "You were the life and soul of the party, and you will be again. Everyone who meets you loves you, there are so many people waiting for you to get your memory back so they can come visit and see for themselves you're okay."

"Really? Why can't I remember that?" She asks sadly.

"You will, I have faith. It may take time, or it may be one small thing that brings it all rushing back at once. You just have to take it steady and try not to put too much pressure on yourself." I reach over and place my hand on hers to comfort her.

Sue slowly turns the pages, examining the pages closely, not just at the people in the pictures but everything around them as well. Occasionally she will point at something and ask a question, something familiar tugging at her memory but not sure what.

I answer everything as best I can without volunteering too much information. The doctor warned us that she needs to remember for herself as much as possible, not have us influence her memories.

When she gets to the photo of her and Smokey on the porch at the ranch she pauses, her hand going to her head, her fingers moving slowly back and forth against her forehead.

"Are you in pain?" I panic. "Do you want me to call the nurse?"

"No dear girl, I'm okay. I just had this really vivid image of me sat on a horse when I saw this picture and I don't know why. I didn't think I could ride." She's still looking at the photo, only now her hand has moved from her forehead to touching the image instead.

I smile widely. "You have learned to ride, and yes, it's where that picture was taken." I hesitate to fill in any more information at this stage. Luckily Sue seems satisfied with that response and continues with the album, occasionally a smile will cross her face, other times she'll ask a question which I answer as generically as I can.

She hasn't quite finished the album when she closes it, apologizing that she's feeling tired again and probably needs a nap. I can't say that I'm not disappointed as she hasn't got to the last photos yet, the ones of the party at Severed MC, but I can't complain, she's made slow, steady progress today and any step forward is to be celebrated.

"It's quite okay," I take the album from her and place it on the table that sits across the bottom of the bed. "You have a nap, and I'll just sit here and read my book for a bit."

Before I've even opened my book Sue has laid back and is already asleep. The doctors had warned us that she'd struggle with low energy for a while yet, and at the end of the day the best cure for anything is sleep, or so Jackson always told me.

I look over at the album at the end of the bed and just hope that flicking through its pages will eventually lead her to remember Jackson. He's lost without her, and I know how much she loved him, it would be a shame to lose that.

I say a silent prayer that this will come to pass, then turn to my book, happy to sit here with her until Eve takes over for the shift change.

CHAPTER TWENTY NINE

Jackson

I close my call with Rebel and can't decide if I'm excited or frustrated, realizing it's probably a combination of the two. Sue is starting to recall some memories from her time here in Maldon, which is great, but she still hasn't remembered me or what we were to each other, which is not great. I just need to be patient, give her the time and the space that she needs. It's just so hard. Part of me blames myself for the accident, if I hadn't broken up with her she might have been with me that fateful day, not on that road and this need never have happened. I know I'm being stupid, but the guilt is eating me up.

"Any news?" Prez asks, knowing it was Rebel on the phone.

"Some stuff is coming back to her from her time here, just little snippets so far, just no memories of me." Prez moves beside me, giving me a consoling pat on the back.

"Progress is progress," he smiles, "shame we're not making any on this trafficking problem. Come on, Declan, Prez and Angel have arrived and are waiting for us." I nod my head, acknowledging his positivity in respect of Sue and sharing his frustration at the problem we're trying to fix.

Once we're all settled around the table in Church, Prez gestures to Declan to start the meeting.

"My contact is as confused as the rest of us, "he starts. "There's just no chatter about trafficking round here at all. It doesn't make sense. If Carnal were involved we'd have heard something by now. There's a task force focused on trafficking and they're coming up blank. There's just no indication of any routes on this part of the coast, or of a new one starting up, it's a good six hundred miles to their nearest known port." He looks around the table to see if anyone has anything to add.

There's nothing, just a lot of head shaking.

"Bert is doing another scheduled run this morning, let's hope they contact him this time, there's been no sign of them on his last two runs." I offer.

"Whatever they're up to its going out, not coming in." Prez adds. "They were specific that Bert took their load on his way to the docks, not bring it back."

"We've had a couple of guys infiltrate the dock and they're not hearing anything either." Declan confirms.

"Let's not forget this is Carnal we're dealing with," Angel joins in. "Since the death of their president they've not exactly been the sharpest tools in the box."

There are murmurs of agreement from around the table. He's not wrong. Carnal is a club in turmoil. There's been so much infighting since the explosion that killed their president, everyone vying for the top spot. The club is fractured, and everyone is at risk of getting caught up in their crossfire.

"What else could they be up to then?" Prez looks around the room for ideas.

No one has been able to come up with anything, so we agree to up the observation, add more bodies to the mix and see if that reveals anything.

Angel volunteers the Severed crew once more to watch the ranch and keep an eye on the creep so we can continue our surveillance of Carnal. He's even stationed one of his guys at the hospital, close to Sue's room, which reassures me. I know his fiancée Eve will have her own permanent body-guard, but it's good to know that Sue, and her other visitors will be safe.

We spend the next hour or two scanning the photos and reports that we've compiled to date, just in case anything jumps out at us but it's a fruitless process. There's no logic or process to the way they've been acting.

Whilst the creep has been hanging around with some of the Carnal gang, it doesn't fit the pattern either. It's been the lower echelons he's had contact with.

"I think it's about time we pick the creep up, the girls are safe at the ranch, and I think we should question him." I offer, "I know just the man for the job." I smile and look over at Wrath.

"What do you want me to do?" He looks to me for clarity.

Wrath left us for a while and joined another club as their enforcer, pretty much becoming their assassin for hire. When we lost Bandit he left them and has been keeping an eye on Smokey ever since. He was pretty much raised by the two of them after his mom passed away. He lost himself for a while, and whilst he's capable of extracting some horrific vengeance, he's still has a moral compass, he needed to know that his work was merited not just available to the highest bidder for the wrong reasons.

I know what he's asking me, not what he should do as much as how far he should go. "Let's make that call once we get the information out of him. It depends on just how deep he is in all of this."

Wrath nods his head to signify his agreement.

There are a couple of murmurs about castrating the bastard round the room, but I know these men at this table, deep down they're good guys and won't extract justice till they know all the facts.

It's agreed that the prospects will pick up the creep. Let's be honest, he'd crap his pants if he saw Wrath, the guy is menacing even when he smiles, which isn't often these days sadly. I know he blames himself for Bandit's death,

Smokey's home burning to the ground and our prospect James almost losing his life in the fire.

"Let me know if you need any assistance," Cam, Declan's right-hand man, offers to Wrath. "I picked up a couple of new tricks on our last mission."

Declan laughs, "Yeah, don't let this guy anywhere near a hot poker! I need eye bleach to get that image out of my mind."

I don't know too much about Declan, Cam and their team other than they're ex-military and came to the aid of Severed when they needed it. I remember Declan and Cam telling me that they'd gone on a road trip after that and ended up saving a girl from a wannabe pimp and sleaze bag.

What is wrong with the world these days? Not only is there no 'love thy neighbor' and every man is out for himself, but they seem to be getting eviler and more despicable every day in the way they treat their fellow beings, using them as commodities, something to bargain with or sell to the highest bidder regardless of the end result. There's so much negativity and fighting and mistreatment. The older I get the more it saddens me. I guess I'm lucky that I have such a close-knit family here at Hellion MC, I have Rebel and my brothers and there are still good guys out there like the guys at Severed and Declan and his Wounded Heroes team.

The room starts to empty as there's nothing more we can do for now till we locate the creep. I turn to Cam and

Declan. "Do you two want a drink? I think I need to hear a bit more about this red-hot poker story."

They both laugh loudly and accept, although they do warn me I'll never get the image out of my mind once I hear their story. Bring it on.

CHAPTER THIRTY

Bert

After losing Charlotte I used to enjoy driving my truck, concentrating on the road helped me not think about the devastating loss. It's only when I'm focusing on driving that my heart has a temporary reprieve from that constant pain. I'm a broken man without her by my side.

Grief is a cruel mistress. One day the memories are so vivid, I swear I can feel her in the room with me, smell that perfume she loved, feel the warmth of her touch on my shoulder. Other days I struggle to recall her face, her smile, the way she'd light up every time I entered the room. She was so much more than my wife, she was my soul mate, and I am lost without her.

I feel like I'm on autopilot when I drive, knowing the route as well as I do after all these years I sometimes lose miles, turning a bend to find I'm much closer to the docks than I thought I was, yet still alert to what is happening around me.

I've barely slept a full night since the accident, knowing that someone almost died because of me, and even though it looks like she'll make a full recovery she's forgotten people who used to mean the world to her. That's on me. It's my fault.

I never once thought that Carnal would hurt anyone but me, and to be honest, death no longer scares me as it's the only way I'll get to see my beloved Charlotte again. I have no one left to lose, but looking at the pain etched on all those faces in that hospital waiting room the other week there is no way I can risk anyone else getting hurt because of me.

I'm torn, if I say yes then how many young girls will suffer, if I say no, how many more innocents will get caught in the fall out. I just have to have faith that the two MC's are right and that they can stop it happening.

I was never able to lie to Charlotte, she used to say my face always gave me away, and I'm scared that when Carnal do come for me again, for I know there is no doubt it will happen, that they will be able to see through me and know that I've been plotting against them.

The rest stop is just ahead of me now and I flick the indicator showing I'm going to take the exit. My heart feels like it's going to beat out of my chest from fear. Despite the familiarity of the rest stop, somewhere I always used to stop on my way to the docks till Carnal scared me away, I still need a moment to sit and calm myself after I take my keys from the ignition.

Drawing in a deep breath I send a silent prayer to Charlotte, asking for her forgiveness and for her strength to get me through this ordeal, just the same as my last two visits through here.

The last two runs were normal, no sign of Carnal. I'm not sure if I'm more scared of them not turning up or seeing them again. I swear I smell Charlotte's perfume fill the cab and there's a warm touch on my shoulder. Deep down I know it can't be her, but I'll allow myself a moment to believe it could be true, to see this as her blessing and a sign she is there for me. A lone tear falls down my cheek, her loss a physical pain in my chest.

Wiping it away, I pull myself together, stepping down from the cab and trying to plaster a fake smile on my face as I cross the car park and open the door for the food stop.

"Bert, great to see you again. Take a seat and I'll be with you in a mo!" Betty the waitress calls out in greeting. She's pouring coffee for some folks seated at a table by the window. I look around the other tables to see if I can see any of the Carnal guys. I see a few familiar faces who nod in greeting, fellow road hauler's and acknowledge them but draw in a breath of relief at not seeing my tormentors.

I take a seat in a booth with my back to the wall and a view of the door so I can steel myself if I see them come in. Betty wanders over, coffee pot in hand and her order pad still in her apron pocket.

"Usual, Bert?" she queries. I smile and confirm that's what I'll have. I've been coming here for years, and Betty knows my order off by heart by now. "You okay, Bert?" Her voice is full of concern. "I heard about that awful accident, and you haven't looked yourself the past few times you've been in. You know it wasn't your fault, sweetie." She puts a reassuring hand on top of mine and smiles warmly at me.

"I, I'm fine, Betty, thank you." I try to smile back at her. "Guess I'm still a little broken up about what happened, and for some reason it has made me miss my Charlotte that bit more." I reassure her.

She gives me a long look, and I'm not sure she believes me until she smiles back, her voice cheery as ever.

"Bless you, Bert. It does get easier, but these things do have a way of coming back and reminding you how much you miss 'em." Betty turns away and goes over to the kitchen window to place my order. She's already filled my coffee cup, and I take a sip of the hot drink to try and settle my nerves. Betty lost her husband Sid five years ago now, so I know she understands what I'm going through. They'd been teenage sweethearts, and she's refused every single customer that has hit on her over the years. She's still a looker, but for her there was only ever one man, her Sid, and she's staying true to his memory, same as me with my Charlotte.

Whilst I know Charlotte would be happy for me to move on and find love again, I can't, and won't, as there could never be anyone who would come close. I'm lost in my memories of her and only notice Betty when she puts the plate down in front of me. I thank her and she's gone as quickly as she came, off to greet and seat some new customers who just walked in. I look up but it's not them, letting out a relieved sigh.

The reason I've been coming here for years is that the food is really good, but today I can't find my appetite, taking small bites but mainly pushing the food around on my plate. I see Betty look over, concern in her eyes, so pick up my fork and take a bite of waffle and bacon. She smiles at me and goes back to serving.

I manage to eat a little more, and drink all my coffee before I rise, leaving the money for the bill and a tip under the coffee mug. I wave goodbye to Betty as I leave and turn in the direction of the restrooms.

As I finish drying my hands the door behind me opens, I look up into the mirror in front of me and my heart drops. It's them.

There are three of them today, one stays guarding the door and the other two approach me from behind.

"Now then, Bert, it's been too long," the ringleader greets me, no warmth in his eyes though, just cruelty shining out. "So sorry to hear about your accident," he places his hand firmly on my shoulder, forcing me to turn round and face him. "That could have been so much worse, couldn't it?" He grins, an evil leer on his face.

I cast my eyes down, trying to calm the nervous shake that has taken over my body. I'm not afraid for me, but I am terrified. Terrified by what this man wants of me, the threat he poses to others and how easily his face lights up when he talks about his plan.

"Now, Bert, I think it's time you and I had a serious talk, don't you." He sneers at me. "And know now, Bert, today I'm not taking no for an answer."

He gestures to his comrade, the one not guarding the door, and he closes in on us, his heavy hand taking hold of my arm and forcing me down to my knees.

"Right, then, Bert. This is what you're going to do."

CHAPTER THIRTY ONE

Jackson

One of the guys has called and confirmed that Bert was approached on his run this morning. I feel a sense of relief that things are slowly starting to move. We agreed with Bert that we wouldn't make contact till he was back from his run to the docks, and only if it was safe to do so.

He's not back yet but he has shadows watching him from a safe distance across the route, no one else has checked in, so we have to assume for now that he's okay.

He's an incredible guy, playing an irreplaceable role and he didn't bat an eye at volunteering. I know from talking to him he's not concerned about his own safety, but that of others, torn between taking part in their diabolical plan or risking more innocents like Sue in the fallout.

I know the accident wasn't his fault, but there's always that moment when I first look at him where all I can see is the image of Sue, battered and bleeding on that stretcher as we carried her to the helicopter.

It's like I'm in a constant state of waiting, frustrated that we can't resolve this Carnal problem and distraught over Sue's lack of memory. I know it doesn't mean that our time together wasn't special enough to her, it's just her bodies way of protecting her, of healing her, but why does it have to take so long, and worse, what happens if she never remembers me. Having it taken almost losing her for me to get my head in the right place to understand just how much she means to me, what if I do lose her because she can't remember me?

I can't afford to think like this. Rebel keeps telling me I have to be positive, small things are coming back to Sue all the time, and I need to remember she's currently having to process losing Elvis all over again, even though she still can't remember that happening.

I glance at my watch and see that Bert won't be in touch for a few hours yet, Rebel is at work, so I decide to hit the gym. I need to release some of this pent-up frustration on the punch bag.

The gym is empty when I get there. Shedding my t-shirt, I wrap tape around my hands. I don't bother with gloves, I want to feel each hit on that bag.

I'm in a world of my own, hearing only the echo of the punch each time my hand hits the bag, not noticing the pain thrumming through my hands, or the blood that is starting to stain the tape. I've lost track of how long I've been here when a hand reaches out and touches my shoulder from behind.

I whir round, fists at the ready and almost hit the guy in front of me.

"Woah there, Jackson," he takes a large step back, "don't be marking this pretty face." He puts his hands up in a gesture of submission before noticing the damage I've done to my hands. "What the fuck, man!" he exclaims, reaching for my hand to examine it.

I flinch and try to pull my hand back, but to no avail.

"You've made a right mess of this," he sounds so disappointed.

"I'm okay," I try and reassure him but as I glance at my hands I know he's right. The skin is badly broken, and I can start to fill the sting of the cuts now. Maybe I did go a bit too far but at least lost in that fugue state I had a respite from all the questions constantly running through my head since the accident.

Aaron shakes his head and looks at me. "Rebel is going to kick my ass when she sees what you've done to yourself." He shrugs. "And yours too, old man." He smirks at that last comment.

Yep, Rebel will not be best pleased.

Before I can defend myself he tells me Bert is on his way

back and we're going to go meet him at the warehouse where he keeps his truck for a debrief.

I give him a look, an unspoken question he answers without me needing to ask it.

"Yep, it's on old man. We're going to get the fuckers that hurt Sue. Now let's get you cleaned up and go see what Bert found out." Aaron hands me a towel to clean the worst of the blood from my hands and we head back into the clubhouse so I can get dressed and treat the wounds.

It still feels weird showering in my room at the clubhouse and Sue not being there when I come out. Her presence still fills the room, thanks to her things still being here. Rebel's offered to clear them out for me, but I keep declining, to me that's like admitting she's not going to come back to me and right now, I refuse to let her go.

I can see it when I look in her eyes that she thinks I need to prepare myself that one day I just might have to. Today's not that day though.

When I'm cleaned up Aaron and I head to the warehouse, Declan, Cam, Angel and Prez are meeting us there. As agreed we park up well away from the warehouse and head there separately. So far the surveillance has shown us that Carnal hasn't been there and there's been no sign of them in the immediate area but it's not a risk worth taking.

When I head through the door Bert is the first person I see, and worry crosses my face. He looks dreadful, like he's seen a ghost. Still, he greets us warmly and lets us know everyone else is here, before passing a curious glance over the bandages covering my hands. I shake my head, letting him know it's nothing to worry about.

We head further back into the warehouse and greet the others. Now that contact has been made we've agreed it's not safe for Bert to come to the clubhouse, we'll have to come to him.

Bert starts off haltingly, it's clear to see he's still shaken by his encounter with Carnal earlier, but as he tells us more of the plan they've come up with the more he becomes his normal self.

They've told him his truck is going into the shop tomorrow for the conversion to be done, and they estimate it will only take a few days, so he'll be back on the road for his next normal run to the docks. When he gives us the name of the workshop Angel seems to recognize it. He's long suspected it's been a chop shop for stolen cars but agrees it is big enough to handle the work to the truck.

Declan reassures us that they won't be able to find the tracker they've installed, its brand-new tech they won't have had access to, and it's not located in an area they will need to have access to for the conversion so we're safe on that score.

When Bert has finished talking us through the information he gleaned from Carnal earlier there's only one thing left to find out. When this is all going to happen.

"They mentioned there were other factors that had to be put in place first," he starts, "but if everything goes as planned it's happening next week."

After waiting so long for something to happen we finally have an end in sight. I almost cheer out loud, the only thing that holds me back is that for this plan to succeed we have to let them take the cargo in the first place. It doesn't sit right with any of us, and we can't guarantee their safety.

What we can guarantee is that we will end this, once and for all. It's been a long time coming but Carnal is going down.

CHAPTER THIRTY TWO

Wrath

I head down to the basement of the old, abandoned farmstead I'd scouted. The creep is already there waiting for me, brought here for me by some of the Severed guys. It looks like they were none too gentle with him as he's semi-conscious, his head lolling on his chest.

He's not aware that I'm here yet. I can't be having that. Part of the reason I am so good at what I do is the fear I am able to instill. That's as important a tool as the blades and other implements I use.

I reach for the bucket of water and toss it over him. It startles him awake, he splutters as he comes to and looks groggily around him. There's not much for him to see as I've kept the lights dim down here, shadows fill every corner. I don't need much light to do my job, just enough for him to see my hulking frame and the tools of my trade, just enough to put the fear of God in him.

I tried hard to leave this life behind me when I lost Bandit, to become the man he believed me to be, so tired of never being sure the punishment I was inflicting was deserved or just bought by the highest bidder. This guy is different. He's been praying on the young, the vulnerable and I have no problem ridding the world of a sickness like him.

At the back of my mind is the knowledge that there is no evidence against him… yet! Before I am done he'll tell me everything he knows, and if he's as guilty as I suspect him to be then I'll sentence him myself.

I still haven't moved, lurking just out of his reach, even though his arms are securely tied to the chair, but well within his line of sight. He finally looks directly at me, and I see him shrink back, fear lighting up his eyes. I know I can be a formidable sight, for many my reputation is enough, but this guy is a nobody, he doesn't yet know who I am and what I am capable of.

I pull up a chair, the back facing him and sit astride it. In my hand I have a knife that I twist and turn, the lamplight behind me catching the sheen and keenness of the blade. It's enough to widen his eyes with fear. Still, I stay silent, which is more than I can say for him. He's blubbering and incoherent. I use the point of the blade to clean my finger-nails, making a point of ignoring him, drawing out the suspense a little longer.

I stand suddenly, kicking the chair behind me and he almost jumps out of his skin. I smell the stink of urine and can see that in his panic he has wet himself. Fucking coward. Moving slowly forward I continue to play with the blade till I'm standing in front of him, placing the knife under his chin I slowly raise his face, so he is facing me, eye to eye, not looking at his lap.

"Open your eyes," I command. He has them squeezed tight shut. When he doesn't respond quickly enough I apply a little pressure to the knife and the point pricks his skin, a drop of blood appearing. It's no more than the kind of nick you'd get from shaving, but he immediately starts blubbering. "Look at me!" I shout when he shows no sign of complying.

Hesitantly he opens his eyes, they're wide and bright with terror, I can almost see my reflection in them. "I'm the monster your mother warned you about, I'm about to become your worst nightmare." I inform him. He tries to cower back against the chair, but his restraints won't let him.

"Now, I'm going to make this nice and easy for you. I'm going to ask you some questions, and you're going to answer them. Do you understand?"

He nods his head, barely. I quickly move closer and his face lights up with fear. "I need your words. Do you understand?"

"Ye..ye..yes." He splutters out. This is going to be too easy. He's an absolute pussy.

"Why have you been following Shelby?" I start with an easy question.

"I haven't!" His protest is too quick, he's not giving this enough thought. Before he's had time to comprehend it I've moved and chopped his little finger off, his hand splayed on the chair arm to make it easier for me. His scream fills the basement.

"This is what happens when you lie to me." I state coldly. "Now unless you want to lose more fingers I suggest you think very carefully about how you answer my questions moving forward." I step back slightly, but leave the knife in his line of sight, hovering above his fingers.

"Why have you been following Shelby?" I repeat slowly.

"Because she's a tease, a harlot. I was trying to find the right time." He has tears trailing down his face. It takes all I have in me not to cut his throat right now, but the prick doesn't deserve a quick ending. I also know there's more to this than he's saying.

I slam the knife down, taking two more of his fingers at the knuckle and he screams out like the little bitch he is. "She's a child you fucking pervert." I say calmly, my face close to his so he can see the disgust in my eyes.

"Why were you meeting with Carnal?" I ask calmly and he immediately tenses.

"They'll kill me, I can't say nothin'." He blubbers.

"I'll kill you if you don't. Sounds to me like you're caught between the devil and the deep blue sea." I move the knife to his neck, applying light pressure which draws a faint line of blood. I swipe the blade, so it wipes up the blood and show it to him. "Now, talk." I don't raise my voice, just speak quietly and calmly.

"I...I...I owe them money. They bought my gambling debt." That's interesting, no one has come up with a gambling problem or debt when they were doing the surveillance.

Suddenly, I put two and two together and really don't like the answer I come up with. I feel sick at the mere thought I've just had, but I'm pretty sure that I'm right.

"And how were you planning to pay that debt off?" I try and calm myself, but anger is flowing through my veins.

"I was giving them Shelby in exchange for wiping out my debt." He hangs his head, I can't tell if it's from shame or fear at what I might do next.

"Who were they selling her to?" I grit my teeth as I ask the question, struggling to restrain myself from lashing out and tearing this fucker to pieces.

"They weren't." He sobs. "They were keeping her for themselves." He hesitates before speaking again. "They told me they'd wipe my debt in full if I brought them a virgin piece of ass, the younger the better."

There's a crunch as my fist connects with his face, breaking his nose. "You piece of shit!"

"I didn't take her! I didn't take her!" he screams out, blood and snot covering his face.

"But you were going to." I slam the knife down on his other hand, severing it at the wrist. I cauterize the wound with the flame from a cooking blow torch, I don't want him to bleed out just yet. It's a neat gadget as I can operate it one handed.

It takes another hour of torture for me to be certain I've got everything I can out of him. By the time I've finished he's a bloody mess, but he's still alive.

"I think we can end it there." I glance over at him, wiping my blade and placing it on the table behind me. There's a flash of relief in his eyes, mingling with the pain he's suffering. He's naive. There's no way this fucker gets to leave here with his life.

Before he's caught up with what I'm doing I've grabbed a different, larger blade, a machete. With one powerful swing I've cut his belly open. He looks at me in shock, then down at the gaping wound. What's left of his hand is still secured to the chair, so he can't try and stem the bleeding, even though it would be impossible.

It takes less than five minutes for him to bleed out in front of me. It wasn't an easy death, nor a painless one. The fucker got nothing less than he deserved.

I clean myself up before picking up the phone to report back to the team. This isn't what we thought it was at all.

CHAPTER THIRTY THREE

Rebel

I'm back at the hospital to visit Sue and I've brought Smokey with me. I know Sue was able to connect with Smokey after Bandit passed in a way that the rest of us couldn't as she understood what it was like to lose your partner.

I'm not sure if Sue is ready to meet anyone else just yet, so Smokey is waiting in the corridor, if I don't call her in she won't be upset, she understands, she'll just go visit James instead.

When I pop my head round the door the nurse is deep in conversation with Sue, and I hear them both laughing. That's a good sign. I wait quietly, not making my presence known till the nurse has finished what she's doing, only then do I greet Sue, giving the nurse a nod of greeting as she heads out of the room.

"That looked like an interesting conversation?" I look at Sue.

"Oh, it was, we were just chatting about the prison break at Barwon, can you believe they cut their way out of the cells." Sue giggles.

"Oh Sue, that was years ago, bless you, but it's good that you remember it." I encourage her.

"Really?", Sue looks perplexed, "I could have sworn I just heard about it yesterday." I don't want to correct her, it feels too much like filling in her memories for her, so I choose to distract her instead.

"Do you think you're up to a visitor, one of our friends from now?" I ask her gently. "It's okay if you don't remember her but she wanted to see you now you're awake." I reassure her.

"I think I'd like that, as long as she understands I might not remember her. I'm sorry, my memories of you are still pretty vague. I keep trying to remember but it just keeps slipping away." I take Sue's hand and pat it gently.

"Don't worry, the doctor did say to try not to force it." I turn and call Smokey in. I'm not prepared for the reaction from Sue when she sees her, but it's a good surprise.

"Smokey! I know you!" Sue greets her with a huge smile, but seconds later the smile falls from her face. "Oh, no, I'm so sorry, I just remembered about Bandit."

Smokey rushes to the side of the bed and hugs Sue carefully, conscious that she's still battered and bruised. "I'm so glad to see you!" Smokey is crying happy tears. What does this mean? She can't really remember me, has no memory of Jackson at all and yet she's remembering Smokey and Bandit.

I'm not sure I should hang around and interrupt this reunion, however, when I suggest I should leave them to it and go visit James, both women shoot me down. I get away with leaving them for a few minutes whilst I pop down to the cafe for some takeaway coffees for me and Smokey, because Sue's had her spleen removed she's not allowed to drink anything but water for now.

Standing in the queue I say a quiet prayer that this might mean Sue will finally remember Jackson. I'm not a religious person normally but feel like I've made up for it since Sue's accident.

When I return to Sue's room I'm pleased to see that they're chattering away like old friends. I look at Smokey, but she gives me a slight shake of her head to show that Sue hasn't mentioned Jackson yet. Oh well, at least she's remembered Smokey for now. It's a step in the right direction.

Sue asks Smokey so many questions which Smokey turns back on her rather than answering directly, with responses such as 'What do you think?" when its anything to do with something Sue should remember. I can see that she is starting to remember more which is good. The temptation to just tell her about Jackson is almost overwhelming but I hold myself back.

"Has the doc given you any idea when you'll be getting out of here?" Smokey asks. It's something I was thinking about as well as Sue doesn't appear to be hooked up to any machines anymore and seems to be in a lot less pain.

"He's suggested I could investigate step down residential care as I have no one at home to support me, or I could carry on with my physio on an outpatient basis. Guess I'll have to consider the residential option as I'd struggle to get back here for appointments, but at least it means I should be getting out of here soon."

"Pfft. You won't be needing residential care at all woman. You can stay with one of us and we'll bring you back for appointments as needed. You should know we take care of our own." Smokey advises.

Sue looks relieved. "That would be great. They've advised it's going to take another few weeks before I'm back on my feet as the op was more invasive than a normal spleen removal. I'm going to really have to watch what I eat and drink as well, there's a long list of things I'm not allowed now."

"Not a problem, you just tell us what you can't have and we'll take care of it for you." Smokey reassures her.

"How long do you have to avoid these foods for?" I ask, I knew Sue had her spleen removed but didn't understand it would cause issues. I always thought it was a useless organ a bit like your appendix, bad enough to kill you if it went wrong but fine to live without.

"It's for life," Sue sighs. "I'll be at higher risk of infections as well, so will be on antibiotics for a few more weeks and need to keep a close eye on it. I'll have to stay away from anyone sick as well. I'm so lucky though, the police told me they didn't think I'd survive that accident, so if this is the price I must pay to still be here, that's fine by me."

We're all quiet for a moment, just thinking about what might have been.

"Hey, enough of that!" Sue calls out. "Let's find that photo album you left for me and have another look at it, see if I can remember anything else." She points to the bedside cabinet where she thinks the nurse has stored it for her.

"What's this?" Smokey questions when I pull the album out of its bag.

"I made Sue an album of some of the good times over the last year or so, see if it helped her memory at all." I offer.

"Oh, what a great idea. Let's have a look then and see which reprobates you remember." Smokey encourages. The first few pages are just photos of Sue but Smokey's eyes go moist when she sees a photo of her and Bandit at one of the events at the ranch.

Sue notices and reaches out to grasp her hand. "He was a good man, and he loved you very much." We sit silently for a moment, each of us remembering Bandit in our own way. It's Smokey who ends it by turning the page.

As we flip through the album it's clear Sue is starting to get her memory back as she recognizes several faces, including Dee Dee and Aaron. This time she doesn't tire, and we make it to the last few photos, the party at Severed with Eve's friends.

One of the photos shows the guys all on the floor being taught some moves by the strippers and Sue startles me by saying she recognizes one of the guys, pointing at Jackson. My heart fills with hope which quickly deflates at her next words.

"He's the guy that was here when I woke up, the one I still don't recognize. Who is he?"

CHAPTER THIRTY FOUR

Eve

Angel has finally talked me into setting a date for our wedding, Xmas Eve. He knows it's only weeks away, but he doesn't want to wait a moment longer than he has to. I can't wait to marry him either, but it doesn't give me much time to plan a ceremony, sort a guest list and find a dress.

I'm also concerned that there's still so much uncertainty about what Carnal is up to. I know Angel too well and he's bound to put himself in danger, it's just what he does. Is this really the right time to be planning a wedding, a celebration of any kind. I can't help but think back to Teresa's wedding, losing her dad, and how she almost lost Prez when Aaron was born.

I know the guys don't go looking for trouble, but when it comes knocking they answer. They protect their own. Being here, I feel part of a huge family, something I always wanted but never had growing up. I feel loved and wanted, again feelings I never had in my youth. That reminds me, I need to send my mother the details so she can get her plane ticket booked.

Coming to Australia for Teresa's wedding changed my life in so many ways. I've found the love of a really good man, a new father for Elizabeth, and even built a relationship with my mother and soon Angel and I are going to welcome our child into the world. I am beyond blessed. It wasn't an easy ride, and I almost died, but I'd go through it all again if it meant I got to keep living this life with Angel.

Elizabeth comes running into the room, she's even more excited and hyper than usual and I wonder if someone has been feeding her sugar. "Mummy, mummy can I be a bridesmaid and wear a pretty dress. Pweees. Daddy said I had to ask you."

Great, I see Angel didn't wait for us to talk to her together.

"Of course you can my gorgeous girl. We need to go shopping so you can pick a dress you like." As expected my daughter knows no patience and wants to go now, right this minute.

"We need to wait for Teresa, she needs to pick a pretty dress as well." I try to calm her down. It's no good. She's halfway out of the door before I've finished speaking.

"I'll go get her so we can go now, mummy!" She screeches with joy as she disappears. I'm not so sure that Teresa will be quite as up for a shopping trip as Elizabeth thinks. It's been a rough time for her with Sue's accident, alongside the memories of her dad it's brought up, and her concern for Prez getting involved in this issue with Carnal.

I feel a flutter and place both hands on my ever-expanding belly. Junior is on the move. I'm sure it's a boy the amount of agro this baby is giving me. Angel says he doesn't care either way as long as we have a healthy baby, but I think deep down he'd like a son.

My eyes are closed as I move my hands over my bump, quietly talking to Junior, letting him or her know how much they are loved and wanted already, when Elizabeth crashes back into the room.

"She said yes, mummy, she said yes!" I'm not sure I have the energy to deal with this level of excitement right now, it's just going to get worse the closer the wedding gets. I wonder if I can talk my mum into coming over earlier to help entertain Elizabeth, it's certainly worth asking.

"And did Teresa say when she wanted to go shopping?" Please let her have answered tomorrow or next week.

"I told her we were going now, mummy and she said yes. She's just getting Aaron dressed." Elizabeth is bouncing on her feet, and I just want to take the weight off mine. Looks like that isn't going to happen any time soon. Taking a deep breath, I push myself up from the chair.

"I guess we'd better get our shoes on then hadn't we." Elizabeth rushes over to me but stops suddenly in front of me. She's trying to be careful around the baby, not that she fully understands it and keeps asking why we have to wait so long for Junior to arrive.

"Can I give Junior a hug?" She beams up at me. My heart melts.

"Of course you can." She approaches slowly and wraps her arms as far as she can around my bump, being as gentle as she can.

"I can't wait to be your big sister, I'm going to love you so much and we have the best mummy in the world, you'll see." She leans forward and kisses my bump. "Mummy, what's wrong, why are you crying? Did I hurt you? Her little voice is full of concern.

"No, my gorgeous girl, these are happy tears. I love you so much." I pull her into a hug, then, wiping my eyes I persuade her we need to go get our shoes on for our shopping trip.

The shopping trip is a success for Elizabeth and Teresa but not for me. There's nothing that sings out to me at all. Because it will be so hot and I'm so pregnant I'm not sure I even want a traditional dress. Teresa doesn't look impressed. I know Angel won't care what I wear as long as I turn up.

My feet are really starting to tire, and my ankles feel swollen, so we find a cafe to give me a rest. Teresa doesn't give in though, continuing to nag me. She gets her phone out and searches pregnancy wedding dresses to show me that I have options. So many of the images seem to be sheer dresses or have the bump on full display, they look more like negligees than dresses. I'm shaking my head when she clicks to the next page and that's when I see it.

It's absolutely gorgeous and I know that's the one I want but the price tag makes me wish I hadn't seen it. It's almost $2000 which is way more than I wanted to spend. With it being maternity, it's not like I can pass it on to Elizabeth either for when she gets married.

"Hang on," Teresa gets my attention. "Look, it says here it can be adjusted on the shoulders and has waist ties, so can be worn when you're not pregnant as well."

I take another look, its ivory vintage lace and has a small train. It looks light and comfortable and has a slip to avoid that awful see through effect most of the dresses we've looked at have.

"If you're really worried about the cost there are sites that will rent you it for about a quarter of the cost," she points to one of the other links on the search page.

I keep flicking through the images and know that this is the one I want. I even love the name of it 'There is only this moment', it just seems to fit perfectly. It's long enough I could get away with comfortable flat shoes underneath it, and I think it would look great with my hair down.

Teresa grins. She knows she's won me over. "Great, that's your dress sorted. Now, let's talk about the guest list!"

CHAPTER THIRTY FIVE

Sue

Today's the day I finally get out of the hospital and it's not a moment too soon. I still can't remember everything, but the doctor isn't concerned, he's happy with how much I've remembered so far and seems confident the rest will come back to me eventually. It's okay for him but it's frustrating as all heck for me. It's like this feeling comes over me, I feel like I do know things, but I just can't get them to the front of my memory, it's there nagging at me but refuses to become clear.

Smokey says that it's just like a more severe menopausal brain fog, and that's bad enough. It's not just a word I can't recall, it's so much more. Some memories don't make sense. I can recall a place, a scent, even the music but the person who was there with me remains just a shadow.

My body still aches everywhere, the bruises are yellow now which is much better than the dark purple I first woke up with. I know I'm lucky to be alive. I've been told that my car has been written off by the insurers, but no one will even show me a picture of what it looks like. They think I'm too fragile but one thing I do remember is how strong I am.

I have to stay with Smokey for a few weeks and I guess it makes sense, but I so want to go home, sleep in my own bed and just have some peace. It doesn't feel like I've been left alone since I came round from the coma and it's driving me crazy.

Don't get me wrong, I know that I love everyone who's been visiting but sometimes you just need some space and to be left alone to lick your wounds. Why, when I think of that phrase does it seem like something I was thinking about just before the accident. I have no recall of the day of the accident at all and only vague memories from the few days before it. yet this sense that I was upset won't leave me. Of course, no one will tell me why or what it was about, the same way that they won't talk to me about that strange guy who was in my room when I first came round.

It's so odd. Whenever I try and raise the subject they change it. More concerning is the way that a little of the light leaves their eyes as they do. It must just be their reaction to the accident I guess. I know that it was touch and go whether I would survive when I was brought in and that must have an effect on them. It scares the heck out of me when I think about it. I know that I wasn't in a happy place, but I also know that I was surrounded by people who loved me and who I loved back.

It hurt when they told me that Elvis had died when I had no memory of that at that point, yet my heart must have known as it was more of an ache than full on grief. I don't think you ever get over losing someone you love, you just get used to living with it. I remember losing my mother and years after still having days where the grief hit so hard it physically hurt. It's always such small things that trigger grief, a word or phrase, a song or even the scent of her perfume and her face is there in front of me, so real I feel I could reach out and touch her.

The doctor has signed me out and all I need now is the meds from the pharmacy and Smokey to arrive to get me out of here. I don't have long to wait as I can hear her cheerful laughter outside at the nurses desk.

She's not alone as she comes into the room, she's accompanied by a porter with a wheelchair. I know in movies this is normally where the patient protests they don't need it, but that's not going to happen with me. I know I'm still unsteady on my feet and welcome not having to try and walk with the stick that the physio has given me.

The nurses all come to see me off and wish me well. They thank me for the flowers and chocolates that I asked Smokey to pick up for me on her way in. They've all been so kind to me and I have seen just how hard they work. They really aren't paid enough for what they have to do and what they have to put up with.

Once the porter has me safely seated in the car he heads to the car boot to load my bags, I have a plethora of cards and cuddly toys from well-wishers. I'm surrounded by so much love, even though I have no family of my own left, I feel like I've been adopted by these two MC club families.

Smokey chatters all the way back to the bungalow. I remember her old house, before the fire, I remember Bandit and how that house was so full of love. I don't remember this new place of hers though. Smokey reassures me that that's because I haven't visited here yet, we normally meet up at the clubhouse or the ranch.

The bungalow is in a stunning location, just five minutes outside of Maldon, but with a creek running through the back yard and surrounded by trees. There's a veranda out front created by an overhanging metal roof. The walls are a mix of mottled red brick and plaster but there's a huge floor to ceiling window and I can see a dining table behind it. To one side a tall brick chimney stands out on the roof and in the middle of the roof is a triangle shaped window which Smokey tells me is for the loft room.

I can see why she chose this property, the location is secluded and peaceful yet close to town if it's needed. "There's more room than I need really," she tells me, "But it means I have room for a guest. James stays in the studio out back when he's not in and out of hospital and the loft room is there for Wrath when he stays. I want him to feel he has a permanent home with me after everything he's been through."

Smokey and Bandit never had kids and it's a shame because it's blatantly obvious this woman has so much love to share. She cares for everyone. When we go inside her home is warm and cozy, the living room and kitchen are almost open plan, separated by a brick fireplace. The interior is darker than I expected as the walls are lined with dark wood cabinets and cupboards.

"I've not got round to decorating yet," Smokey reflects as she looks around the room. "It's a bit too dark in here for me, I'd like to keep the exposed brickwork but swap out the dark wood for something more like light oak, a bit more modern."

Her old farmhouse was such a welcoming home with light, bright colors. This place looks cozy, but I can tell it will look so much better when she finds time to put her own mark on it. The guest room is comfortable, a double pine bed with a light floral-patterned comforter, a ceiling fan, bedside tables and a matching double wardrobe. There's even a comfortable chair positioned next to the window, the fabric matching the comforter. It looks perfect for relaxing in with a good book.

Smokey helps me over to the bed and I lay down on top of the comforter, exhausted by just that short walk from the car. Once she has me settled she brings me a glass of iced water and some pain meds.

"I'm going to let you rest now, I'll wake you in time for supper," she promises, "then we can see if you feel up to visiting the ranch tomorrow or if you'd rather stay here."

I was fine until she mentioned visiting the ranch then my heart rate shot up. It's like I was afraid of the ranch for some reason. What on earth is there about the ranch that would make me feel this way? I told myself I was just being silly, it's just my exhaustion, and the increased pain from moving around but in the back of my mind there's that shadow again, that person I can't quite remember. Do I know him from the ranch? No matter how hard I try I can't make the memory any clearer. I guess only time will tell, and perhaps a visit to the ranch as Smokey suggested. We'll have to wait and see.

CHAPTER THIRTY SIX

Jackson

I sit on my bike and watch as the light turns off in Smokey's guest room. Part of me knows that this is wrong, that I am stalking the woman I love, but another part of me can't bring myself not to be here, to keep watch over her. There's this fear deep inside of me that something is going to go wrong and that I can't protect Sue.

I know it's illogical and that having broken up with Sue, I have no right to be here. But the heart wants what the heart wants. She may not know who I am anymore, or want to get to know me, but I can't stop the feelings that I have for her. I will always regret the decision that I made to break up with her.

I feel my phone vibrate in my pocket and pull it out to see who is calling. Shit, it's Smokey. I have a feeling I've been rumbled and I'm not wrong.

"She's okay, I've got it from here." Smokey reassures me when I pick up the call, not giving me time to speak. Before I can respond she's hung up on me. Damn that woman and her intuition. I need to trust her. I know she'll take care of her. I allow myself to linger a little longer and feel my phone vibrate again. I'm in for it now. Smokey is going to give me hell, yet when I check my phone it's not her. It's the clubhouse.

"Jackson," I answer with my usual brevity.

"Get here as soon as you can, it's on." Another call that hangs up on me before I have chance to speak. Finally, something positive, it feels like we've waited forever for things to start moving and yet the timing sucks. As much as I want to stay here and keep an eye on Sue I know I need to get back to the clubhouse.

I'm the last to arrive and when I enter Church I see everyone from Severed is here as well, most of them standing around the room as there aren't seats for everyone, I nod to Declan and Cam who are leaning against the far wall then spot Bert at the table. He looks dreadful, I don't think I've seen him this pale since the night of the accident.

"Now that everyone's here I'm going to hand over to Bert so he can tell us what happened earlier and why we've called you all here tonight." Aaron kicks off the meeting.

Bert is nervously wringing his hands, and his voice breaks a little when he first starts talking but he soon pulls it back. He goes on to tell us that Carnal reached out today and told him tomorrow's the day they need him to take the cargo to the docks.

They won't confirm what the cargo is, he's on a need-to-know basis. As far as they're concerned all he needs to know is where to be for the pickup and where to go for the drop off.

'So, once the cargo is loaded they trust you to get to the docks on your own?" Cowboy is surprised.

"They warned me they'll have eyes on me, so I guess that means they'll be watching from a distance on the route." Bert confirms.

"This either means they're very clever or incredibly stupid." Declan enters the conversation. "From everything we've seen I'm going to go with a combination of stupid and a lack of manpower."

"Carnal isn't that small a club," Angel confirms. "They may not have the numbers they had when the old Prez was alive and my brother was their VP, but they still have enough bodies as far as I'm aware."

"I think this is a side operation, probably not sanctioned by the club, a few rebellious members trying to strike out on their own." All eyes turn to Declan, I guess he could be right. It could explain why everyone has struggled to find out information on this plan of theirs. "Do you have the destination where you're supposed to drop off yet?"

Bert shakes his head. "They've told me to meet them just here at five am" he indicates a spot on the map. It's a secluded location and there's nowhere for us to hide without being spotted. The good news is that we know their ultimate location, even if we don't know exactly which dock and ship the final destination will be.

Declan continues, "We have the tracker on the vehicle but by the time that gives us the information that we need it will be too late to get bodies on the ground. There aren't enough of us to cover every opportunity and whilst they can get a team up here in time, again we don't know where to deploy them. Let's not forget we're only supposed to be supporting the authorities, not taking the lead."

There's a moment whilst we all digest this, I can see everyone thinking, trying to come up with a solution.

"Assuming they're going to take Bert's phone from him can we hide one in the cab somewhere?" I miss whoever calls that out, must be one of the Severed guys as the voice isn't familiar.

It's decided that would be too much of a risk. We don't want to do anything that would put Bert at risk and whilst we know that this band of Carnal renegades might not be the sharpest in the box we really can't risk it. I suddenly have a thought.

"Bert, didn't you say you used to be in the Naval Reserve?" I think I may have something that might help us. Bert answers in the affirmative. "Do you know morse code?"

"Yes, how does that help us?" Bert looks curious.

I take hold of the map and indicate a junction a little further on from the Carnal meet up point. "If one of us was to sit here you could signal us the dock number, you'll know it by then and it should give us enough time to get in place before you get there."

"That might work," Declan agrees. "Sometimes the simplest solutions are the best ones. Let me see what we can get sorted, hopefully we have enough advance notice."

Declan gets on the phone to his contact, and between them they come up with a plan. I can only hear one side of the conversation and get a bit concerned when Declan starts to raise his voice. "That isn't going to work, mate. You wouldn't know anything about this without these guys. You can't leave them out of this. It's not fair, they're too involved." The conversation goes back and forth for quite a bit longer, it's hard to hear what is being discussed at the other end and all Declan seems to be doing is making noises of agreement, a 'yeah', 'huhuh', 'okay'. I can only hope it's positive, I really can't tell from here. The call continues for what feels like forever, the room around us is getting restless. Guys are shifting and fidgeting in their seats and Bert is looking particularly uncomfortable.

"Okay, we're sorted, see you in a few." Declan ends the call and turns to face the room, everyone stops what they're doing and sits straight.

"Guys, we have a plan, pull your chairs in and pay attention, because this is how it's going to go down."

CHAPTER THIRTY SEVEN

Sue

T he sunlight coming through the window is dappled thanks to the trees outside, making patterns on the light quilt that is covering me. It felt so good to sleep in a real bed after the confines of the hospital, just not quite as good as being able to sleep in my own bed. Still, if this is the only way I can escape that place I am grateful for Smokey's hospitality.

I stretch as much as I can with the various aches and tensions in my body. There's something about the way the light is hitting the room that tugs at my memory. I strain to recall it, yet it remains elusive, an echo of a man's laughter is all I can manifest.

Sometimes, the more you try and force a memory the harder it is, I can hear my mom telling me the best way to find something you've misplaced is to stop looking for it and thinking about it for a few minutes and you have more chance of remembering where you left it.

I smile softly as I think of my mom, her hugs, her laughter, her occasional disappointment during my rebellious teenage phase and I get a warm feeling. I wish she was here still, I could really do with one of those hugs right now.

Jackson used to tell me that as long as you remember your loved ones they are never truly gone. Wait! Who's Jackson? Where do I know him from? Trying to force my memory won't do any good, I can already feel the start of a headache behind my temple. I look for the glass of water I know was on the bedside earlier and see a handful of pills atop a handwritten post it note next to it. It's from Smokey reminding me to take my medicine when I wake. She has been so good to me. My heart hurts for her loss. I still feel grief for Elvis, but we were only together for such a short time compared to her life with Bandit. My grief feels raw and fresh, yet I know Elvis wasn't a recent loss. I know I mourned him and that I moved on, moved away, this grief feels more recent. I reach out and try to interrogate the feeling. Somehow, I don't think its related to someone passing, it's not as deep, not as cutting as that but it must be a loss of someone important. My instinct is that this is a person, someone who was special to me and then wasn't, someone that has been lost to me.

It's no good, all this is just making my headache start to pound. Pushing myself up into a seated position, I grab the tablets and swallow them down quickly. A faint hope that this will ease my head as well as the dull ache that seems to encompass my whole body. I feel very old and fragile right now.

I'm unsure what the schedule is for my hospital visits, I was too eager to escape there to focus on when I'd have to return but I know Smokey took careful notes. I think I have a reprieve today, I'm sure Smokey suggested something about just taking it steady today. I hope so. It would be nice to just sit on a chair outside in the sun today, it feels like forever since I enjoyed some fresh air.

My bladder reminds me that I need to find the bathroom, I'm pretty sure it's through the living room and off the kitchen. At least my hospital room was ensuite, this is going to be a long walk compared to the last few weeks. When I rise to my feet it takes a moment to steady myself, more from the unfamiliarity of standing for so long, rather than the dizzy spell that I had feared might happen.

I take it steady as I make my way through the house, I can hear Smokey in the kitchen singing along to an oldie on the radio. She's singing loudly enough that she doesn't hear my soft shuffle across the tiled floor, startling when she turns suddenly and spots me, dropping the cutlery she was holding which clatters to the floor.

I'm not sure which of us shrieks the louder, me or her. I'm just grateful I didn't wet myself with the shock. "Why didn't you call me?" Smokey chastises me. "I'd have come and helped you."

"Because I'm not a baby!" I feel my face flush with embarrassment at the harshness of my tone and instantly apologize to her. "I'm so sorry. I'm okay, honestly. I just need to start doing things for myself, get back to normal. I'm tired of being looked after."

Smokey huffs out a breath and comes towards me to give me a hug, she's gentle but it still feels comforting. I enjoy it for a few moments then my bladder reminds me why I am up and about.

"I really need to go to the bathroom before I make a mess on your floor, I'll be right back." I promise as I slowly extract myself from Smokey's arms. Smokey guffaws with laughter and lets me go.

Having relieved my bladder, I return to the kitchen. The aroma of fresh coffee and bacon and eggs greets me. Smokey gestures for me to take a seat and brings a steaming mug of coffee over to me. I can't avoid the moan of pleasure that escapes me when I take that first sip. That tastes so good, I hadn't realized just how much I missed it in the hospital.

"It's decaf coffee and the bacon is turkey bacon, I've scrambled the eggs so there's no risk of them being raw at all. Do you think you could manage some?"

"I'm not sure I'm that hungry," I feel guilty when she's gone to all this effort for me. "Could I just have a little?" I offer a compromise.

Smokey nods her head and turns to the stove, plate in hand. "The doctor explained you should eat little and often, don't worry. I've got this."

When she returns to the table with two plates I see that she's having the same as me, she just has a little more on her plate. I'd lost my appetite in the hospital and remember the really bland, soft food I was on for the first few days. I'm still not sure I have any appetite now. I don't want to offend Smokey, so I take a small bite of the eggs and they're delicious. Having food that isn't bland does make a difference and I slowly enjoy my breakfast, although I still have to leave some on my plate, unable to finish it.

Smokey doesn't look disappointed like I thought she would, just congratulates me on being able to manage as much as I did.

"That's good progress," she encourages me. "Now, what would you like to do today, I was thinking you might like to sit out back on the veranda and enjoy some fresh air."

"You're a mind reader. That would be perfect, thank you. Although, I would like to get dressed." I gesture at my nightwear. "It would be good to feel a bit more human."

"I'm sure you'd enjoy a nice shower as well, there's plenty of hot water so take as long as you need. Do you want any help washing your hair?"

I reach a hand up and feel my hair, it does feel a bit greasy and unkempt. Just touching the hair at my shoulder has caused my wound to pull and twinge so I know I won't be able to do it myself. As much as I'd like to have clean hair I'm not comfortable being naked in front of Smokey in the shower. I somehow managed to handle the lack of dignity in the hospital, but now I'm out it's very different.

Smokey senses my hesitation and offers encouragement and a potential solution. "If we pull a chair up sideways to the walk-in shower do you think you could hold on and lean back a little, would that work for you?"

"That would be wonderful, thank you so much." I'm beyond grateful to Smokey for her kindness and compassion, not to mention her generosity in letting me stay here.

We sit at the table a little longer, enjoying our coffees before heading to the bathroom. Smokey helps me position myself on the chair so that I am comfortable.

The sensation of the warm water on my hair is wonderful and as Smokey massages the shampoo into my scalp I feel myself relax into the experience. This feels so good. As she starts to rinse the lather from my hair a memory hits me suddenly. This feeling, this same sensation but it's not from here and now, and the hands in my memory are stronger, calloused, masculine. I can't see who it is yet, but I know it's someone that I love and trust, someone I am familiar with sharing a shower with me, both of us naked, washing away the traces of our lovemaking.

I'm a little embarrassed to be here with Smokey while I have this flashback, but I try and hold on to it regardless. Then it hits me full force, I know who is in the shower with me. It's Jackson!

No sooner has his face filled my memory than the rest of it painfully resurfaces. As Smokey conditions and then rinses my hair I stay quiet, unable to voice the hurt that suffuses me. My heart feels like its breaking.

"There we are, how does that feel?" Smokey asks me, carefully wrapping my damp hair in a towel. As she comes around in front of me she notices the tears falling down my face. "What's wrong? I didn't hurt you did I?" She looks distraught.

"No, it wasn't you." I reassure her. "It was Jackson. I remember him."

Smokey looks like she's about to clap her hands in joy but stills them quickly as I finish what I was saying.

"I remember him, and I remember him leaving me and breaking my heart."

With that I break down into sobs so violent they shake my whole body. Smokey wraps her arms around me, trying to comfort me but it barely helps at all.

I look up at her, hardly able to focus for my tears. "I wish I'd died. Why did they have to save me?" I howl.

CHAPTER THIRTY EIGHT

Jackson

Bert was nervous when he set off this morning, who can blame him. This crazy situation is out of my league as well. I just hope that everyone manages to get in place early enough to avoid causing any suspicion.

Even though I know deep down it wasn't Bert's fault that Sue got hurt, there's a part of me that still blames him. Fuck, there's a part of me that blames myself as well. If I hadn't broken up with Sue she might not have been on that road that day. If this, if that, it might be, it might not be. The words seem to echo around my mind on a constant loop. I really need to get my head in the right place, I can't let the side down today.

Something still doesn't sit right with this whole situation, the truck has been converted for trafficking, but we can't work out where the girls have been taken from, where they've been kept or who the buyer is. There are still so many unknowns. It's so far outside of what Carnal have done previously, organizationally that is. Don't get me wrong, they've done some pretty evil shit but nothing on this scale and with Satan and Prez out of the picture Angel feels strongly that they wouldn't have the intelligence to plan something on this scale and get away with it.

Regardless of what any of us think, shit will be going down today. Time for me to get on my way.

I meet up with the rest of the guys about ten minutes from the dock at a disused warehouse, arriving just after the call has come through that the action is going to be happening at dock 7. That makes sense as it's one of the more remote docks and should be less populated.

"What's sailing from there today?" I look around the group.

"Word has it that it's a trawler heading to Russia." Declan advises, then returns to a phone call I hadn't spotted he was on.

Cam hands out some earpieces, I look mine over amazed at how small it is. This is all new to me. He gestures to some unlocked secure boxes and tells me to help myself. They're full of weapons, handguns, knives and automatic rifles as well as a shit load of bullets. I already have my Ruger 9mm with me but take a couple of spare clips. I know Aaron has his Glock, he says its more accurate, but I guess it's a personal choice, I prefer the trigger pull on mine.

We're both ex-military but normally only use our guns at the range behind our clubhouse. We carry them for defense rather than offense normally. Guess it's lucky we practice at least weekly, more for competition than anything. I'd say friendly competition, but I think it's just a little more serious than that. I smile to myself knowing that I'm currently just ahead of Aaron on the scoring with only a few weeks left till Christmas. I've a good chance of winning. There's a grand on the table for the winner. I'm not that fussed about the money, just the bragging rights that go with it. It's how we both roll and why we're such close friends.

Declan gets off the phone and heads back over to join the rest of us. "Listen up everyone, we need to work out our plan now we know the location. The fact the Russians are involved means we need to really be on our top form. A couple of the guys on the ship have been identified as Russian Bratva, they're highly trained and lethal. We hadn't expected them to be involved as they have other, more lucrative routes for their trafficking. Declan's contact has sent us a couple of snipers which we can use on the higher positions, but I'd be happier if we had someone on that crane over on the left of the ship as well. Anyone got any experience?"

Aaron steps forward, "It's a while since I did any sniper work, but I was pretty good back in the day. I can certainly be a backup." Declan asks him a few questions and seems happy that he can do the job, especially when Aaron finds the model of sniper rifle he's familiar with in amongst the inventory.

Once we've all donned bullet proof vests, the rest of us are allocated positions either in nearby cargo hangers, or at various points along the dockside. We have plenty of time but want to ensure that we get in place and out of sight well in advance of Bert's arrival and before the day workers start to arrive.

"Let's have a comms check." Cam starts off and each of us checks in. When everything is confirmed to be working correctly we set off in small groups. There are a couple of entrances to the docks, and we've been told which one each of us needs to use.

It's still early when we get there so the sun hasn't risen yet, but it's not far off. It would have been better if we were doing this in June when the days are shorter rather than now when they're at their longest, allowing us that little bit more opportunity to make use of the dark.

That's something else that isn't computing, why the hell are Carnal pulling this off in daylight. They're either incredibly clever or ridiculously stupid. I have a feeling it's not going to be as easy as them being stupid, and we already know they have no morals or social conscience so this could go badly for us. Still, it's a risk we're all prepared to take.

We're all in our positions well before the sun rises, and we still have a half hour before Bert is due to arrive and drop off his load. It's been agreed he'll move off as soon as it's done so he can make his regular pick up on time. At least we'll know he's safe.

The plan is that Carnal will be there to unload his truck, with help from some of the guys on the trawler which hopefully means that Bert will get away safely. We need to make sure we take them all down today, not only to save the girls but also to make sure there will be no one to come back at Bert later.

There's a quiet voice in my ear asking each of us to check in and I respond as quietly as I can when it comes to my turn. It's not escaped my notice that my guys and the Severed guys are on the outskirts of the action and it's Declan and his contact's teams that are positioned in the riskiest locations. It makes sense I guess as they're the more experienced amongst us, despite our own military pasts it's been some time since any of us have been in this kind of situation.

The waiting seems interminable, and definitely longer than half an hour, but eventually I hear the signal to say Bert has passed into the docks and is on his way. I double check my Ruger, for probably the tenth tine since I got into position and make sure the spare clips are easily accessible.

I can just about see the trawler from here and as the sun rises I can see several armed guards patrolling on there. Shit just got real.

CHAPTER THIRTY NINE

Jackson

I still can't believe what went down. We couldn't have been more wrong. Carnal weren't trafficking girls at all. We'd all been so tied up in Sue's accident and the aftermath that none of us had been paying attention to the news.

We'd stayed hidden whilst Carnal and the Bratva guys boarded the truck, realizing that there were still more armed guys left aboard the trawler, and we didn't have an ideal route to get to the truck ourselves without them seeing us. I could hear Declan and Cam strategizing over the earpiece. The snipers were tasked with taking out the armed guards on the trawler, freeing several of us up to approach the truck.

We didn't want to put the snipers into action too early, risking our plan being blown, but we also didn't know how long we had before they started unloading. The next thing

I knew Cam was tasked with belly crawling towards the rear of the truck. Man, he has some balls on him. The snipers were briefed to keep an eye on the armed guards and take them out if any of them spotted Cam. He would signal as soon as he heard signs of them having opened the hidden compartment and moving the girls to the rear of the truck.

Cam would signal twice, once to advise they were on the move, and the second to let us know how many prisoners he could identify. We'd already counted the number of Carnal and Bratva aggressors who had boarded the truck, there were four of them on there in total. It had been agreed he would signal via clicks rather than speaking so there would be no risk of him being overheard. There was a fair amount of noise already in the air as cargos were being loaded and unloaded on other docks, but it wasn't worth the risk.

I think we were all thrown when only two clicks came through for the number of girls. Nowhere near as thrown when six men jumped down from the back of the truck, where the hell were the girls?

In addition to the Carnal and Bratva guys we'd already seen there were two huge guys wearing jeans and black leather jackets, both carrying large black holdalls. What the fuck was going on. It was Aaron who spotted who they were via his sniper scope.

"Fuck, that's Bob McAvee. I thought he was serving life in Barwon?" His voice whispered over the earpiece.

It took only seconds for Declan to respond, "He was broken out last week, along with another inmate doing life." Declan pauses, I assume he's checking for further intel. "The other guy is Visya Ivanov, nephew of the head of one of the Bratva families." There were several whispered curses in my ear when Declan interrupted. "The plan hasn't changed. We take out the guards and we detain the cargo, only difference is this cargo is likely to fight back."

Everyone acknowledges his instruction and awaits the go signal which comes through just seconds later. I feel a healthy apprehension about this change of events. I never anticipated I'd be going up against the Russians this morning. Those guys are brutal. That's why Ivanov was serving life, he'd brutally murdered his mistress for nothing more than answering him back. He'd done it in front of witnesses, confident that his family connections would ensure he would get away with it, that their billions would buy his freedom. Well, looked like he'd got his freedom now, but he'd had to serve six years of his sentence to get to this point. McAvee was an MC enforcer who'd only been sentenced a few months ago, I'm only guessing that was where the Carnal connection came in.

All of this was rushing through my mind whilst I was moving into position. Out of the corner of my eye I see the guards on the trawler go down. The snipers have taken them out, but it doesn't take long for replacements to come running up on deck, they quickly fall as well.

The others have just dismounted off the back of the truck when Cam and several of his team move into sight, having been hidden out of sight down the side of the truck till then.

Despite being surrounded everyone from the truck pulls a weapon and starts shooting. It feels like it's all blowing out of control. Bert puts his truck into gear and blasts out of there, despite the rear doors still swinging wide open. I don't blame him, I just hope he doesn't get caught up in any crossfire.

I move as quickly as I can, my gun drawn and aimed. I see one of Cam's team go down and take the clear shot I have at one of the Carnal scum. He crumples to the ground, my bullet having hit clean between his eyes. Ivanov realizes the gunman at his side has gone down and looks in my direction. The last thing I see is his gun aiming at me before I feel a searing pain in my chest, as I hit the ground everything goes black.

Fuck, my head hurts. It takes a moment for me to work out where I am as the last thing I recall is the shootout at the docks and I don't remember there being any pillows there. I feel a pillow under my head. As my vision comes back into focus I start to recognize my room at the clubhouse, although there's barely any light in here. Can it be evening already?

I try and shift on the bed and feel a soft hand easing me back down. "Shhh, just lay back, you took a nasty knock to your head. Let me tell the doc you've woken up."

I do as I'm told, closing my eyes and hear footsteps head toward the door, the door open and whispered words I can't quite grasp. The steps come back to the bed, and I feel the mattress sag a little as someone sits down beside me and gently smooth their hand against my cheek.

That voice, it can't be, as much as I want it to be, I must be dreaming. I risk opening my eyes again and look up at Sue's face. "What? How?" I barely croak out, quickly followed by an apology. "I'm so sorry, I was an idiot, please don't go. I need you."

Sue reaches over to place her finger on my lips. "Shhh. You need to rest. As soon as I heard that you were hurt I had to come, even if you didn't want me here, I had to see for myself that you were okay. I love you, that never changed. Yes, you were an idiot, but you're my idiot and I'm not going anywhere. You can't get rid of me that easily."

I let out the breath I'd been holding and reach for her hand, clasping it tightly. Before I can say anything else the door opens, and Doc comes bustling in.

"Ahh, I see you've decided to re-join us. Gave us a bit of a scare there." He goes on to explain that the force of the bullet hitting my vest had thrown me backwards and I'd hit the ground hard, knocking me out. I'm going to have some bruising and tenderness from where the vest took the impact, and I'll probably have a stinker of a headache but he's confident I'm going to be okay. I refuse to get checked out at the hospital so Doc agrees I can stay here as long as someone is with me overnight to keep an eye on me. I was right, I've been unconscious most of the day, it's almost midnight now.

Sue offers to stay with me and my heart fills. Am I getting a second chance here?

As Doc starts to pack up Sue lets me know that I have some people who really need to see me just to reassure themselves that I'm okay. She promises they'll only be here for a few moments as she'll kick them out if they don't leave. Doc has barely got out of the door before Rebel comes rushing in, followed by a worried looking Aaron.

Sue lets them both know I'm okay and Doc is happy for me to stay here, emphasizing that I need to get some rest. Rebel has her hands moving all over me, trying to reassure herself I really am okay I suspect.

Aaron clasps my free hand and squeezes it. "Glad to have you back, gave us a bit of a scare there."

"What happened? Is Bert okay?"

Aaron starts to fill me in, ignoring the disapproving look from Sue, and says he'll give me the detail tomorrow, but the plan worked. Bert is safe and Ivanov is back behind bars. McAvee didn't make it, but that's no real loss.

Sue turns to Rebel. "See, I told you there'd been a prison break, I heard it on the radio."

Rebel laughs and reaches over to hug Sue. "I'm so glad you're back with us. We've all missed you." She looks at me.

"We've missed you more than you'll ever know. Can you ever forgive me?" I beg.

"I think I could be persuaded," she laughs and her whole face lights up with her smile.

She starts to usher Rebel and Aaron out of the room.

"Off with the two of you now, we have to let him have some rest." It takes a few moments to persuade Rebel to leave, but eventually she does, promising to be back early in the morning.

"Not too early, we have a lot of catching up to do here." Sue grins.

Sue locks the door behind them and comes and lays beside me on the bed. "Now, get some rest. You can show me why I should forgive you when you're feeling a bit better."

I pull her in closer so I'm spooning her. The last few weeks have been a hell of my own making, but it looks like I might be getting a second chance. No more regrets.

CHAPTER FORTY

Rebel

After the stress of the last few weeks, I can't believe it's Christmas tomorrow, with everything else going on it kind of snuck up on us. I'm looking forward to today though, a celebration of love is exactly what we all need right now.

We've been invited to Angel and Eve's wedding over at the Severed clubhouse and we've invited them all over to our clubhouse for a Christmas day barbecue tomorrow. It feels like we're all one big extended family now, and that makes me happy. Sue was the common factor that brought us all together and I am so relieved she is back on her feet and more importantly, back with Jackson.

It's a shame that it took both being hurt to shake some sense into their heads, but it seems to have worked. The only thing not perfect today is Chris, he's been antsy the last few days and I can't get him to tell me what's wrong. I thought things would get better after Declan introduced him to his colleague who promised to take care of the searches so that his dad's ill-gotten gains could be returned. With the resources they have the search will take a lot less time and it means that Chris can spend more time helping at the ranch, allowing me to start on some of my ambitious expansion plans.

I'm not going to let this spoil Christmas though, I'm determined that I'm going to enjoy the next few days with friends and family, and we can sit down and talk it out after. Today is Angel and Eve's day after all.

In keeping with the family vibe, it's not going to be a church wedding, they're getting married out back at the clubhouse. The setting is stunning. There are white chairs on both sides of an aisle, and at the bottom of the aisle there's a pergola adorned with white roses, sprigs of holly add a dash of greenery and there are stunning baby pink blush peonies to create highlights.

We're sitting on the brides side as Eve has no family here other than her mother who has flown in from England and her daughter, Elizabeth, who will be her bridesmaid. The Severed guys are on Angel's side. Prez is Angel's best man and they're both stood at the front laughing and joking, no nerves at all.

I understand that their friend Cowboy will be doing most of the speaking at the ceremony, with the celebrant doing the legal bits. He'd wanted to do the whole thing but apparently it would have taken a full year for Cowboy to obtain a registration, and they didn't want to wait that long. This way they have the best of both worlds.

They're all wearing black jeans, white shirts with open collars and their club vests. Angel has a large pink peony on his vest and Cowboy and Prez have white roses. They scrub up well. Chris looks less than amused when I voice that thought out loud, giving me the side eye. I laugh out loud and give him a peck on the cheek. He's looking pretty hot himself, beige linen trousers and an open white shirt, but I'm not going to tell him that just yet.

Sue and Jackson arrive, and Sue takes the seat next to me, I greet her with a warm but gentle hug. "I'm so glad to see you back up and around." I take hold of her hand and squeeze it. "You scared the heck out of us there. I'm even more pleased this great lummox saw sense and you two are back together again." Jackson gives me a disapproving look, but I know he's not serious. He knows what an idiot he was already, he doesn't need my constant digs. I might start letting him off the hook in a few days but right now it's too much fun pulling his leg.

Sue had rushed straight over to the clubhouse as soon as she'd heard he was hurt, we all had, but Sue was the only one allowed in to see him that night. Doc had advised more than one visitor was too much and we all agreed that it was Sue he'd want by his side when he woke up. It didn't mean the rest of us hadn't stayed there all night waiting for him to wake up, then sleeping there so we could see for ourselves the next day that he was okay.

A rush of affection comes over me and I reach over and squeeze his hand too. "You know I love you really," I reassure him. He gives me that amazing smile of his and my heart is full. I'm sat here surrounded by family and friends and I have everything I could want. I'm one of the lucky ones and I will never let myself forget that.

Music has been quietly playing in the background whilst we all got seated but now it changes. Shania Twain's 'From this moment' starts, the volume now louder and the words make my eyes start to leak. What a perfect song for a wedding ceremony.

Cowboy asks us to all stand for the bride, we not only stand we all turn and crane our heads for that first sight.

Teresa is the first to approach the aisle, she looks stunning in a long, burgundy sheath dress with tiny straps and a low-cut neck. Her dark hair has been pulled up, tendrils falling either side of her face and there are small pearls dotted in her hair. She has her hand loosely placed behind Elizabeth's shoulder, guiding her. The little girl is adorable, her own dark hair is hanging in curls and she's wearing an antique style flower girl dress in white, a sheer gauze covers the shift dress underneath and ends in a border that falls below the shift and edged with lace and embroidery. In her hand she has a basket and is tossing rose petals everywhere and very randomly but the smile on her face is huge, her eyes are bright, and she just radiates happiness. As they arrive at the front Teresa is pulled into a passionate kiss by her husband, and Elizabeth runs over to Angel grabbing hold of his legs and beaming up at him.

"Look, Daddy, I'm a flower girl!" Everyone laughs at her enthusiasm. "Wait till you see Mummy," her voice loud and full of glee. "She looks so pretty."

"So do you, darlin," Angel leans down and kisses her on the cheek. "I'm so lucky, I get to celebrate today with my two best girls."

Teresa eventually persuades her to move back over to the bride's side and we all turn back to await the bride. There's an audible gasp as Eve comes down the aisle by herself. She looks absolutely radiant.

Her dress is an antique embroidered cream lace that trails along behind her with a tiny train. It's covered in geometric lace patterns and falls beautifully around her baby bump. There are sleeves but they're split in such a way they fall behind her arms and leave her shoulders bare other than some delicate straps. As she draws close I can see that the dress is split to her thigh but falls in such a way that the two sides sit over each other so all you can see are her calves.

She's holding a bouquet full of roses and darker pink peonies, their stems all visible and bound together with hessian string. The overall effect is stunning, but I have to laugh when I see her shoes, she's wearing comfortable cream trainers covered in bling. You go girl!

The look on Angel's face when he sees his bride is awesome, you can see that she has taken his breath away, and his whole face is lit up with love. I think every woman wishes for a man who looks at her like that at least once in her life. You can tell just looking at them together when Eve arrives at the front that this isn't a one off. This man loves her like this every day, and one look at Eve's face tells us all that the feeling is mutual.

Sue reaches over and touches my hand, when I look down she is handing me a tissue, her other hand is wiping tears from her eyes. I take the tissue realizing that there are happy tears streaming down my own face. Being here, in this moment, and sharing this special experience with Angel and Eve is priceless and beyond heartwarming.

The official registrant is warm and welcoming and has personality but it's nothing to Cowboy when his turn comes. I see now why they wanted him to do this, when he talks about the happy couple his love for them shines bright, leaving us all in no doubt how much they both mean to him. I love that he includes Elizabeth in his speech, blessing the family they are now and the family they will become when Junior arrives. When he speaks it turns the day from being simply a wedding to something so much more, a joining of a family unit, not just a couple.

There's the loudest cheer as they are pronounced man and wife and a flurry of rose petals are thrown over the happy couple as they run back down the aisle, Elizabeth in the middle of them.

What a perfect service.

The rest of the day was even more relaxed. Whist Angel insisted on caterers being brought in so that everyone could enjoy the day fully and we all sat in a huge U-shaped set up, white cloths on the tables, glass champagne flutes, toasting the bride and groom who were seated at the table at the top of the U shape. The food was delicious and very simple. A huge bar was set up on the side with bottles of iced beer for the men and plenty of spirits for anyone who wanted them, along with a bartender to make fruity nonalcoholic cocktails for the bride.

Alcohol flowed freely as did the laughter, an area had been set aside as a dance floor and the DJ played something for everyone, the dance floor always full and those who preferred not to dance happily drinking, laughing and just celebrating.

I'd been sitting with Chris, Sue, Jackson, Smokey, James, Wrath and Maeve. Chris was enjoying himself but still seemed a bit antsy to me and I could swear Jackson had started with it too. Wrath was his usual brooding self and ignoring Maeve's obvious attempts to get him on the dance floor. Bloody men!

'A Little Respect' by Erasure came on and I dragged Sue and Maeve onto the dance floor with me, the guys having refused to join us. What a surprise...not. As the song ended the music stopped and we all turned to the DJ stand wondering what was happening. We'd already had all the toasts.

Jackson and Chris were stood in front of the DJ stand, and I wondered what they'd asked him to play. It wasn't like them.

"Right, everyone, we have a special request, and with the permission of the bride and groom I'd like to ask Sue and Rebel to stay on the dance floor and dance this next one with their partners, if everyone else could sit down."

I look at Sue and she's as confused as me. Eve and Teresa are giggling away as though they're in on the secret, in fact, looking round the room it looks like pretty much everyone apart from us is in on it."

I give Chris and Jackson a piercing look, but they just smile nervously and reach for our hands. As our hands join the music starts. It's quite a poppy intro and feels familiar but I can't quite place. I know it's Bruno Mars though. Something about a beautiful night. Just as I work out what the song is and as the words 'Marry You' are sung both Jackson and Chris fall to one knee and open small velvet boxes showcasing sparkling rings. The music level drops.

I'm not sure which of us is the most shocked. Chris lifts the ring from the box and holds it up to me. "You are the missing part of me, Rebel, the one I want to spend the rest of my life with. Will you marry me?"

I'm nodding my head like an idiot but can't get the words out.

At the same time Jackson is telling Sue how stupid he was to ever think he could live without her, how much she means to him and asks her to marry him.

We both finally manage to blurt out the word yes at the same time and the music goes back up to full volume as the rest of the guests cheer. We're surrounded by well-wishers and Eve and Angel are the first to congratulate us.

"You knew?" I question Eve. "But it's your day?"

"Of course we knew, and it's the perfect ending to our special day." Eve hugs me warmly, followed by Angel.

I'm still in shock, I look down at my ring finger and see the diamond sparkling back up at me, not even knowing when Chris managed to place it on my finger. I guess this explains his behavior the last few days.

Chris pulls me into his arms and kisses me deeply, when we part I look around me, seeing everyone who means something to us here, in this place, and we are surrounded by love.

I think it's safe to say this is going to be the best Christmas ever!

EPILOGUE

Rebel

Christmas seems like a distant memory already, every time I look at my engagement ring I'm reminded of what an amazing time it was. Christmas day at our clubhouse was as full of love, family and friendship as you could ask for.

After the engagement ring I hadn't expected a gift from Chris, but he surprised me with an amazing holiday. He's booked us a two-week cruise to New Zealand next month and I cannot wait. He wanted us to spend some quality time together, just the two of us, after all the stress we've been through. I'm looking forward to it as I've never been on a cruise and never visited New Zealand either.

I think Sue was rather jealous and poor Jackson is trying to come up with a suitably impressive holiday for them. It's so good to see them so happy together. As much as it annoys Jackson, Sue is still staying with Smokey, it's easier for her hospital check ins and she's decided she wants to sell her house so they can buy something together. Somewhere that is theirs. It's going to be hard to let go of my family home, where I grew up, but the memories will always be there, and there are as many here in the clubhouse I guess. It's the right thing for them though.

Chris is more than happy for us to stay in my little house, although he did mention we would need to extend when the kids come along. That threw me as it's not a conversation we've had before, but part of me is glad that's the kind of future he sees for us. I'm not ready for that yet though.

Work has already started on the renovations at the ranch and I'm so happy we're going to be able offer hope and support to more kids. I can't wait for Maeve to get here so I can offer her a full-time position at the ranch so she can get away from the bar job she dislikes. It should mean she can spend more time with Wrath as well. We can all tell that he loves her, but he hasn't caught up on it yet himself, meanwhile she's in love with him and it's currently unrequited. I have hope that they'll get their happy ever after as well though.

Eve and Teresa are here already, we're meeting up to open the DNA results. Teresa didn't need to take a test as she knows who her family are but wanted to come give Eve some moral support and is curious what hers will show about where her ancestors came from. Prez is convinced there must be some warrior tribe in her background to explain her temper. The results all arrived in the post the last couple of days, and it's been killing me not opening mine already.

Poor Eve looks like she's about to drop any moment, although she still has a couple of weeks to her due date. The summer weather hasn't helped, and the poor girl keeps saying she looks and feels like a beached whale! Bless her.

Eve and Angel aren't going on their honeymoon until after the baby has arrived and is a few months old as they wanted to travel as a family. They're going to visit England and do the tourist thing. Eve's mum will look after Elizabeth and the baby for a few nights to give them some real alone time but will be traveling with them to help the rest of the time.

It's been great to see Eve rebuild the broken relationship with her mum, it's so very different to the one she had during her childhood. I guess there's a comparison there between me and my mom, I didn't know who she was until I was thirty and wasn't sure I wanted to know her for a long time, but we're building a strong relationship now.

Everyone had laughed at the DNA kits I bought for Christmas and there'd been lots of debate about where we might have originated. None of us have done family trees at any point and depending on the results of these tests I guess that's something we could explore. Jackson didn't have a clue, but Aaron's face was a picture when he opened his. I think he'd truly convinced himself I wouldn't want to know. We both know it won't change the way I feel about Jackson, he always has been and always will be who I think of as my dad, but I think it would make Aaron happy if he knew, once and for all, one way or the other.

Aaron and Jackson are off entertaining Elizabeth whilst we open our envelopes. I think they understood how much this might mean to Eve and Maeve, and I appreciate their compassion.

Maeve bustles into the clubhouse, hot and flustered. Her boss had needed her to work extra and made her late. She comes in with a barrage of apologies, hugs and kisses.

Once we're finally all settled with drinks and envelopes we look at each other.

"Who's going first?" Eve asks, a tremor in her voice.

"Why don't we all do it at the same time?" I suggest. Everyone nods in agreement, and I give us a countdown. "On three, one, two, three!"

I hesitate a moment longer than the others before I open my envelope. Looking around no one has torn the envelopes, they've all opened them carefully, almost respectfully.

There seem to be a lot of pages, and I skim the first few, they talk about things like geographical background, character traits and then I find it, the last page showing me my DNA matches. I draw in a breath when it shows what I guess I already knew. I leave the rest of the pages to review later.

Teresa is laughing at hers, she mutters that Prez will be happy that she has some Viking blood in her veins. Eve looks disappointed, sadly her result hasn't found a match with her father.

"Not yet anyway." Eve tries to sound positive. "It doesn't mean I won't find one as more people take the tests."

Maeve however is sitting there with her mouth open, shock written all over her face and muttering to herself.

Just then the door opens and Aaron and Jackson walk in with Elizabeth. Aaron looks over at me and I nod my head just enough to let him know he was right. That's going to be an interesting conversation later.

I turn to ask Maeve what she found but she's oblivious to the rest of us around the table, her eyes focused on the men in the door.

"I don't believe it," she waves the papers in the air in the direction of the doorway. "You're my father!" she points.

TO BE CONTINUED in the next installment of Hellion MC

WRATH

A HELLION MC NOVELLA

AVA MANELLO

PREVIEW - WRATH

Wrath

I roll my shoulders, trying to ease the tautness between them. It's been a long day. The ache doesn't lessen, not that I really thought it would, I really put my back into today's job. The knot just to the side of my neck is solid against my hands. A hot shower should help, and if nothing else, I need one to clean the splattered blood from my skin and hair.

Tossing my red checkered shirt into the trash can rather than the laundry bin as I'm never going to get the blood stains out of it, I pause for a moment and take note of my reflection in the mirror. I barely recognize the dark lifeless eyes that stare back at me, hell, I barely recognize me anymore. My dark hair is a little too long on top and has started to give in to the natural curl that I hate, although my mum always told me it was a kiss curl and she loved it. The shaved sides are growing out and my beard needs a serious trim as well, I'm starting to look like a dark-haired version of Santa Claus albeit with a six pack instead of a belly, although it's safe to say there's nothing good and giving about me. I've been on the road for what feels like forever. That said, when I look through the door to my bedroom here in the clubhouse, I have to ask myself am I really home? I'm more nomad than brother these days, a club enforcer hired out to the highest bidder to do the dirty work no one else wants or has the stomach for.

Constant raging anger fills my veins, fueling the work that I do. Every job takes away a little more of the humanity I once had, turning me into the numb shell that's looking back at me in the mirror. I've never questioned that my victims are guilty, I trust that my Prez has done that already. I just carry out the sentence. I walk in, mete out the punishment requested of me, then walk out, leaving someone else to clean up behind me. This is what my life has become. I feel more like a machine than a man these days, and I can't see that changing any time soon.

Life was good once upon a time, I even vaguely remember the sound of my laughter, but that's in the past. A twist of fate and that life was gone, leading me to become the man that's standing here today. A man without a soul or a conscience.

My brothers in the Club embraced that change. They take pleasure from the fact I am filled with anger, hate and violence and I use that to fuel the vengeance they ask of me.

Easing off my leather boots I place them carefully on the floor, before removing the rest of my clothes. I grab a clean towel from the pile on the shelf and place it within reach of the shower door.

The steam from the hot water flowing from the shower head fills the small ensuite, my skin turning red from the punishing heat, the water swirling around the drain is deep scarlet with the blood I'm washing away from my body. It's not my blood, it never is. I'm too good at what I do. It's the blood of yet another poor soul who was found wanting and deserving of punishment.

Closing my eyes, I can still hear the man's voice pleading for forgiveness, his last words full of fake apologies that mean nothing to me. He means nothing to me. He's just another name on a piece of paper that needs to be crossed off so that I can move onto the next one. I don't ask what any of them have done because I really don't care. I can hazard a pretty good guess that this time it involved taking or touching something that didn't belong to him just from the punishment I was asked to deliver.

The heavy meat cleaver I'd asked for had been there waiting for me when I walked into the room, the victim already there and strapped into a chair. The whole scene had been set to ensure he felt the maximum amount of fear. The naked, dim bulb swung slowly above his head, casting moving shadows around the room. There was no requirement for bright lighting or a clean environment, this was no surgical procedure I was about to perform. The damp walls and dirt covered floor merely enhanced the night-mare ambience of his situation.

I don't know how long he'd been sat there for, restrained, and awaiting my arrival, staring at that cleaver whilst working himself up into a state of terror, but I do know that he recognized me as soon as I walked in. My reputation already preceded me. I could see the resignation and fear in his eyes as soon as he realized it was me. I'm an imposing figure even in a normal setting, my six-foot four height often has me standing a full head and shoulders above my brothers. I'm not overweight, instead I'm toned and solidly built. In this setting I must have looked like an avenging angel to him, and I guess that's all that I am these days.

Feeling the heavy weight of the meat cleaver I turned it over in my hand. It was already well used; the blade had recently been keenly sharpened but the hilt had multiple nicks and scratches that betrayed its age. Avoiding looking at the prisoner I stood there for several long moments just turning and inspecting the weapon I was holding, deliberately stretching out the anticipation and terror I was sure he was feeling.

With one deft stroke my work was done, the strike clean, leaving his hand severed at the wrist. Nevertheless, blood still spattered everywhere. I turned my back on his high-pitched screams and walked slowly and steadily away from him and towards the daylight. It wasn't often a victim's screams followed me as I left a scene, more often than not the silence of death filled the room instead. This guy was lucky, not that he'd see it that way for a while I suspect, but he'd been allowed to live. I often wondered why they brought me in for this simple kind of job, but my Prez had once told me it was because of the effect the sight of me walking into a room had on a victim. My reputation was enough to fill them with terror, and they'd believe I was there to snuff out the life someone else felt they no longer deserved.

It didn't matter to me one way or another, I had a job to do, and I did it. That was my life now.

The water finally runs clear, so I pick up the shower gel and liberally apply it to my body, working up the lather and cleaning off any remaining evidence of today's labors. When I'm done here, I'll grab something to eat from the kitchen as I realize I haven't eaten all day, then I'll go see my Prez and find out what vengeance I'll be dishing up next and who to, because that's my job. This is my life, it's the only one I know now, the only one I dare remember. I can't afford to remember a time before this, when compassion was a part of me, when I had a soul. I can't be that man anymore. Too much has changed, too much has happened that cannot be undone.

I am sin.

I am Wrath.

Read More

ABOUT THE AUTHOR

Ava is a passionate reader, blogger, publisher, and author

who loves nothing more than helping other Indie authors publish their books be that reviewing, beta reading, formatting or proofreading. She will always be a reader first and foremost.

She loves erotic suspense that's well written and engages the reader, and loves promoting the heck out of it for her favorite authors.

STALK AVA MANELLO

Ava Manello Reader Group (Facebook)
https://www.facebook.com/groups/613212832386624

Ava Manello Facebook Page
http://www.facebook.com/AvaManello

Ava Manello Website
http://www.avamanello.co.uk

Ava Manello Threads
https://bsky.app/profile/avamanello.bsky.social

Ava Manello Blue Sky
https://bsky.app/profile/avamanello.bsky.social

Ava Manello Instagram
https://www.instagram.com/avamanello

Ava Manello BookBub

https://www.bookbub.com/authors/ava-manello

Ava Manello Newsletter

https://geni.us/AvaNewsletter

ALSO BY AVA MANELLO

Rebel (Hellion MC 1)

This is not your normal MC story.

Abandoned at birth, Rebel has been raised by the men of Hellion MC. Happy and successful, living the life she's chosen outside of the MC, everything changes when her mother surfaces on her 30th birthday, desperate to forge a relationship with her daughter.

All is not is as it seems.

Duplicity and betrayal threaten not only everything she holds dear, but her very existence. Forced to decide between the mother she's always wanted and her MC family almost destroys her.

Who will she choose, and who will she lose?

Wrath (A Hellion MC Novella)

When rival club enforcer Wrath is asked for help, he is torn between doing what's right and stirring up a past that still haunts him.

What follows is a journey that forces him to question and re-evaluate everything he thought he already knew.

Decisions have to be made.

Should he continue on the path he's chosen or is there a chance of becoming the man his mother would have wanted him to be?

Life doesn't always have a happy ever after, no matter how much you want it.

This is a heart-wrenching tale of heartbreak and loss.

Be warned, it will leave your emotions in tatters.

Declan (Wounded Heroes 1)

War almost destroyed them, but they survived thanks to their brother in arms Declan. Coming home wasn't as sweet as they'd hoped, lives had moved on without them. For one it was all too much. United by grief and angered by injustice the Wounded Heroes vow to always be there for each other. Little do they know that's going to come sooner rather than later.

Can be read as a standalone or as part of series.

Cam (Wounded Heroes 2)

Fate's been cruel to Sarah Kennedy. Not once, but twice, her future has been altered by the turn of a card. Believing she's been abandoned by everyone she cares for, and barely holding on to her sanity, she finds herself caught up in a battle of wills between two men.

Luckily for her one of them is Cam. He vows to keep her safe from harm. Little do they know how hard that promise will be to keep. With no hope of escape Cam calls on Declan and his fellow Wounded Heroes for assistance.

What follows is a crazy, violent adventure that could cost them all their lives. But then, these are the Wounded Heroes, and they've never shied away from a conflict before.

Can be read as a standalone or as part of series.

Strip Back (Naked Nights 0.5 Eric's Story)

Strip Back brings you back to how the Naked Night's began. This is Eric's story. Back when life was a little less polished, and a whole lot harder.

Before there was Strip Teaser, there was Eric; manager and founder of the Naked Night's male stripper troupe.

You wouldn't think you'd be past it at 34, but that's the position Eric found himself in, as well as newly single after finding his girlfriend in a compromising position.

Setting up the Naked Night's wasn't easy, it wasn't fun, and it wasn't without sleaze, but somehow he did it.

Strip Back is a humorous and steamy tale of one man's journey to fulfill a dream. Not all male strippers are the same.

Strip Teaser (Naked Nights 1)

When investigative reporter Sally Evans receives her latest assignment to uncover the naked truth, she gets more than she bargained for.

Eight weeks on tour with the Naked Nights male stripper troupe to expose all their dirty secrets, is this serious reporter's worst nightmare. She'd rather a man keep his clothes on. For Sally, sex is only a consideration if it happens in the dark, not that she can remember the last time she had a reason to turn the lights off.

With over-eager, over-sexed female fans in abundance and baby oil by the gallon, the guys are looking forward to some fun.... Sally's inhibitions are not.

Strip Down (Naked Nights 2)

What happens when sexy British male strippers head to Australia on tour and meet the hot bikers from Severed MC? You'll be crying with laughter as they try to teach the Severed guys a few moves to impress their women… outside of the bedroom for a change!

Catch up with some of your favorite characters from Naked Night's and Severed MC. Alongside some sizzling new dance routines there'll be lots of love, laughter and possibly even a few happy tears in this novella.

The 'Non' Adventures of Alice the Erotic Author

It's a laugh out loud collection of coffee break reads with a touch of kink!

There's a bit of Alice in all of us. She's just an ordinary girl, trying to get through each day, and encountering a few humorous pitfalls along the way.

Alice is an erotic author with a vivid imagination, which she puts to good use for her readers.

Follow Alice as she goes from hot fantasy to crashing back to earth when her flights of imagination evaporate into a disappointing reality.

From everyday encounters at the gym or tattoo shop, to a rendezvous via a dating site.

You just know the reality is never going to match up for poor Alice.

Severed Angel (Severed MC #1)

Eve lived a very boring, very vanilla life with her boyfriend and two year old daughter.

After the douchebag left her, leaving her a penniless single mum, her best friends wedding in Australia came at just the right time. She's missed her childhood friend, Teresa moved to the Aussie sun with her widowed father when the girls were 18, meeting her biker lover out there and now Eve is set to be her Maid of Honor.

Instead of having the much needed break she's looking for, she witnesses a crime that puts her life in danger. Her dream vacation just turned into a nightmare, something she has only read about in the books she loves to escape in.

Being rescued by Severed MC turns out to be an experience. The clubs VP Gabe aka Angel, could be just the diversion she needs right now but, no matter how hot the tattooed biker is in and out of bed, she still misses her daughter back in England.

Book One in a two part story.

Carnal Desire (Severed MC #2)

Continuing Angel and Eve's story from Severed Angel.

Eve returns home unaware danger is hot on her heels. Will Satan get the revenge he seeks, will Angel save the woman he loves or will Ink get the woman he deserves.

The nail biting conclusion to the story that crosses two continents...

Book Two in a two part story.

Severed Justice (Severed MC #3)

Your favorite Severed MC returns with more chaos, more danger and more fireworks.

Satan may be gone but the danger isn't.

With revenge on the cards from more than one player and hot blooded new comer Justice stirring things up, the people in the town of Severed are in for one hell of a ride.

Carnal Persuasion (Severed MC #4)

The fourth installment in the Severed MC series finds Cowboy wrestling with his demons. Can he go on, or is he too broken after everything he's endured?

Meanwhile the citizens of Severed are caught up in a war, and it's down to Severed MC to try and save them.

This book is going to blow your mind.